Caught Up

BY

SHANNON
HOLMES

Infamous

This is a work of fiction. All names, characters, places, and incidents are a product of the author's imagination. Any resemblance to real events or persons, living or dead, is entirely coincidental.

Published by Akashic Books
©2015 Shannon Holmes

Hardcover ISBN-13: 978-1-61775-375-6
Paperback ISBN-13: 978-1-61775-374-9
Library of Congress Control Number: 2014955756

Infamous Books
www.infamousbooks.net

Akashic Books
Twitter: @AkashicBooks
Facebook: AkashicBooks
E-mail: info@akashicbooks.com
Website: www.akashicbooks.com

Also Available from Infamous Books

The White House
by JaQuavis Coleman

Black Lotus
by K'wan

Swing
by Miasha

H.N.I.C.
by Albert "Prodigy" Johnson with Steven Savile

Sunfail
by Steven Savile

CHAPTER ONE

A light rain began to fall upon the Washington, DC metropolitan area, ruining what had been an unseasonably warm spring day. The National Weather Service had issued a storm advisory for the area. Quickly the precipitation went from a random shower to a steadier downpour, which led to torrential rain and high winds that battered everything in their path: highways, homes, pedestrians, cars, and whatever else was not shielded from the elements. The fury that Mother Nature had suddenly unleashed caused many drivers to panic and pull over to the side of the road and wait out the storm. Only a few dared to keep driving in such horrible conditions.

The HID lights from the pearl-white Range Rover Sport shone brightly into the ominously darkened skies, slicing through rain, giving its driver decent visibility—much more than the average vehicle on the road. The Range Rover cruised along the flooded downtown streets of the nation's capital, finally making its way onto Interstate 95.

At the wheel of the luxury SUV was Bryce Winters, a transplanted native New Yorker, along with his girlfriend Dixyn Greene.

"I told you it was gonna rain," Bryce said calmly without taking his eyes off the road.

"You did," his girlfriend admitted meekly. She knew this was coming. From the time the first raindrop had hit the windshield, Dixyn Greene knew he was going to say something. This was a pet peeve of his. When Bryce was right and she was wrong, Dixyn was going to hear about it.

"I said let's do this tomorrow or on the weekend, but no. We could have turned up this weekend instead of havin' one funky-ass rainy day."

Dixyn peered through the passenger window onto the soaked highway; everything was a blur. She was focusing on nothing in particular; Dixyn just wished to avoid the mean stare that surely accompanied Bryce's lecture.

"How many times have I told you when it's goin' to rain?"

"A lot," Dixyn mumbled.

"And how many times have I been wrong?"

"Never."

"Well, until I lie to you about that, believe me! I got a muthafuckin' bullet in my body. You know I can tell when it's goin' to rain before the weatherman can."

Dixyn had heard enough. She turned to face him. "Well, what gives you such mystical powers that you can forecast the weather?"

SHANNON HOLMES

"Oh, you tryin' to be funny? *What gives you such mystical powers that you can forecast the weather?*" he mimicked.
"This lead in my shoulder! That's what."

"Bryce, why you yellin'? It's not that serious."

"To who? Speak for ya'self."

Fuming, Dixyn went silent again and resumed looking out the window. She noticed that the vehicle was
crossing the bridge into Virginia, which meant they
would be home in a matter of minutes. Finally she said,
"Bryce, you really know how to break a bitch down. You
know that, don't you? Babe, today is my birthday. Could
this please not be one of them times? Let's just drop it."

Up until this point, Dixyn had been enjoying her
birthday with her significant other. It was a date filled
with good food, good music, and good company. It
wasn't often that she got a chance to spend time with her
man outside of the house. Bryce's lifestyle, much like his
mood, was unpredictable. Such was the life of a hustler.
His late-night runs and trips to New York to re-up were
the norm in his line of work.

Nonetheless, Dixyn knew the benefits outweighed
the drawbacks by far. Going without seeing her man for
days on end was a small sacrifice to pay to live in the lap
of luxury. Bryce was a good provider. Dixyn didn't want
for anything while he was around. All she had to do was
ask, and the item in question usually came into her possession. Dixyn had a brand-new black BMW X6 parked
in her garage, courtesy of Bryce. The couple also had a
beautiful town house in the suburbs of Alexandria, Virginia. Several prominent members of the government

were rumored to live in their development. Bryce's dirty money had introduced Dixyn to a lifestyle that she had previously known little to nothing about. And now she had grown accustomed to it.

Aside from his covert drug dealings, Bryce was usually a good father and a good man, though was not without fault. He had his moments. He could be a real asshole when he wanted to be. He had an uncanny knack for making a big issue out of the smallest thing. Yet there was little doubt in Dixyn's mind that she had chosen the right man not only to be her mate, but to conceive her child with. Her daughter was well taken care of and Dixyn was more than thankful for that, especially with all the baby-daddy nonsupport drama that some of her girlfriends from high school were currently experiencing. Bryce had no other children, so there was no crazy other baby mama, there were no thirsty tricks calling him at all times of the night, and, as far as she knew, Bryce never stepped out on her. And if he did, he sure hid it well. All Dixyn knew was that he loved her. She felt it. He showed and proved it in special ways, all the time.

Aside from all the material possessions he showered her with, nothing quite comforted Dixyn like Bryce's presence. Dixyn agonized over his absence whenever one of his trips out of town kept him away from home for more than the allotted time. In the darkness of her room, on her loneliest nights, Dixyn cried for Bryce, longed for his touch, and she always prayed for his swift and safe return.

Now Bryce glanced down at the speedometer and

eased off the gas pedal. He hadn't realized he was going so fast. With the limited visibility and vast amount of falling rain, these were extreme weather conditions. To avoid hydroplaning on the slick highway, Bryce exercised some common sense. He wanted to arrive home just as he had left: in one piece. As the vehicle gradually slowed down, Bryce cautiously maneuvered the SUV into the right lane, preparing to exit off the highway.

Dixyn took the initiative to break the tension that had built up inside the car. She reached over and gently squeezed Bryce's muscular arm. Her touch conveyed more than words ever could. It said, *You won; I don't want to fight anymore.*

Wisely, Bryce decided to let it go. He knew the best part of being with Dixyn was coming home and going to bed with her. He knew if he pressed the issue any further it would mess up the mood. Dixyn wouldn't sex him to the best of her abilities. Even worse, he might have to sleep on the couch.

"I'm sorry, babe," she said affectionately. "You still mad at me?"

Before he could respond, a small grin creased his lips. This expression seemed to say it all. It communicated to Dixyn all that she needed to know. "Nah, I was just sayin' . . ." Bryce began in his heavy New York accent. "Sometimes, ma, you gotta listen to the kid. I be knowin' what I'm talkin' about. Facts! We both know how you can be, though. You want what you want, when you want it, regardless of the circumstances surrounding the situation."

It was Dixyn's turn to smile. Bryce understood her

all too well. At times when they fussed and fought, Bryce referred to her as a big baby, and she agreed. She knew this character flaw was unwomanly. While she had tried to change, she just couldn't. It was who she was: spoiled. Her entire life her mother had given in to her. Being the only child raised in a single-parent household, Dixyn grew up with the misconception that she could go through life always getting her way. Bryce was guilty to a degree of facilitating this by spoiling his woman with expensive gifts. But, of course, she would never see it like that.

"Babe, look, I know I can be on my bullshit at times. But whenever I get a chance to be with you, I'm going to take it. I don't care what the circumstances are. I don't care if the world is coming to an end. Let me be right here with you when it does, and if I die, I'll know I died happy." Dixyn Greene was a hopeless romantic. When it came to true love, she was a believer. She stood firm in her belief that she had found her soul mate in Bryce. The connection she felt from the moment they met still existed to this day, despite their occasional disagreements.

"Wow," Bryce managed to say. He was blown away by Dixyn's sincerity. How could he knock her just for wanting to be with him? What man in his right mind could? Bryce was overcome by a warm fuzzy feeling inside—it was good to know that his woman wanted him just as badly as he wanted her. At that moment, words couldn't express how he felt for Dixyn. Bryce took his eyes off the road long enough to quickly admire her. He had run through many women in his day but, he had to admit, he had lucked out when he got with Dixyn.

They were from two different worlds. Bryce hailed from the rough-and-tumble concrete jungle of New York City. His Harlem neighborhood served as an incubator for drug dealers, spawning some of the most notorious in the city. Dixyn was from suburban Virginia, unaccustomed to the fast lane. She wasn't about that life. Her naïveté to the street life played a major part in his initial attraction. Opposites attract—bad boy from the bright lights and big city, and the good, wholesome suburban girl. The two met by chance while Bryce was on a shopping spree at a local mall and they immediately clicked. They had been inseparable ever since.

Dixyn was everything he wanted his wifey to be. She was an incredible mother, a straight-up freak where he needed her to be, and she was absolutely beautiful. Dixyn had a natural prettiness which other women envied. She hardly ever wore makeup; she didn't need it. He liked that. Everything about her was real, from her hair and nails to her breasts and ass and, above all, her character. Dixyn was the only female Bryce had ever really loved, the only woman he was even remotely faithful to. She had a good heart. She was trusting, almost too trusting at times, naive to the games of the trifling broads always sniffing around her, the ones she called friends— the same ones who sometimes made passes at her man.

Her childhood best friend Kendra was the main culprit—the two had recently gotten back in touch with one another and Kendra would often make inappropriate comments about Bryce. She was just too loose when it came to sex. She was in love with a new guy every other week, constantly giving up the pussy. Dixyn made it a point to never discuss her relationship with Bryce, sexual or otherwise, with Kendra. True, Kendra played an important role in her life, but relationship counselor wasn't part of it. As good as Kendra looked, Dixyn never understood why she couldn't get a decent man. Her life was a never-ending cycle of bad relationships, one after another.

"Must be nice," Bryce blurted out to break the silence.

"What?"

"Always getting ya way." He smiled.

In response, Dixyn playfully punched Bryce in the arm. She liked his sense of humor. He could be a clown when he wanted to be. Dixyn rested her hand on Bryce's inner thigh and slowly massaged through his jeans until she reached his erection. "It's on when we get home, baby," she joked as she worked to unzip his jeans. "I want to show you how much I love you." Dixyn gently released Bryce's manhood and tenderly kissed the tip. "And how much I missed you." She used her tongue to tease the length of his hardness. "How much I love you," she whispered before taking his fullness into her mouth.

Bryce was so overcome by the strong warm sensation that he almost forgot he was driving. "Chill, you gon' make me crash my whip."

Dixyn came up from her bowed position in his lap and smiled wickedly. "I'ma fuck the shit out of you when we get home!"

By the time the couple arrived at home, the rain had subsided. The glow from the moonlit sky illuminated the path to their driveway. Instinctively, Bryce surveyed his surroundings. His eyes scoured the area for would-be intruders or anything else that seemed out of place. Bryce was security-conscious. He could never be rocked to sleep by the slow country atmosphere of the suburbs. He treated every day as if danger abounded.

Satisfied that nothing was out of the ordinary, Bryce pressed a button on the Range Rover's sun visor that activated the two-car garage door, revealing one empty space and Dixyn's BMW X6. As soon as the Range Rover crossed the garage's threshold, Bryce hit the button again and the door closed behind them.

When the couple entered the house, the home security alarm sounded. Bryce rushed over to the keypad and punched in a code, switching the alarm into a home mode, which meant that the couple was free to wander about the house, but that if any doors or windows were breached, it would chime again.

Bryce entered the living room and walked over to his well-stocked minibar. He grabbed a bottle of Hennessy cognac, his drink of choice, from the bottom shelf and followed Dixyn upstairs into the bedroom. Bryce removed the top and took a hard gulp. Although he was accustomed to drinking Hennessy straight, the burning sensation made him grimace. Regardless, he took another long swig, followed by another. He repeated the process until he reached the bedroom. Satisfied that he had consumed enough alcohol to enhance his sexual performance, Bryce placed the remnants of the Hennessy bottle on the nightstand.

The faint sound of running water told Bryce that Dixyn was already in the bathroom taking a shower. His timing couldn't have been better. He opened a drawer inside the nightstand to ensure that what he had planted before they left for an evening on the town was still there. The small black suede box was right where he had left it. Bryce removed the item, carefully placed it inside his pocket, and closed the drawer. While Dixyn freshened up in the bathroom, he rehearsed the plan in his mind. Bryce was nervous, but not noticeably. The large amount of alcohol he had just consumed helped calm his outward appearance. This moment was a long time coming; he had finally worked up enough nerve to do the right thing by not only his woman, but his child as well. Dixyn had held him down through the good and bad, she had his back through thick and thin, he had started referring to her as *Wifey*, and now he wanted to make it official. He wanted that commitment for life. Bryce was confident that the label wouldn't complicate things. Rather, marriage would enhance their relationship.

The sound of the bathroom door opening snapped Bryce back into reality. He looked up just in time to see Dixyn slowly approaching him, wearing nothing but a white towel which covered her breasts and her upper thighs. As soon as Dixyn came within arm's reach, she seductively let the towel fall to her beautifully pedicured feet, revealing her perfect figure.

Slyly, Bryce let his eyes roam over every inch of Dixyn's body as his manhood rose to a rock-solid position in his pants. Her sheer beauty justified Bryce's attention. The sexual overtones in the bedroom grew stronger when Bryce reached for her small waist and pulled her close. He tenderly planted soft little kisses on nape of her neck, sending shivers down Dixyn's spine. This was her spot and Bryce knew it. Not quite ready to jump into a heated sexual episode with his woman, he pulled away, ceasing all stimulating activities.

Bryce looked deeply into Dixyn's eyes and smiled. His expression was so warm and alluring that Dixyn couldn't help but smile too. He kissed her softly on the lips, then softly said, "You know I love you . . ."

"I love you too," she whispered, and kissed him again long and slow. For her, there was nothing more erotic than a passionate kiss.

Bryce knew exactly what Dixyn's slow kisses entailed. Slow kisses led to slow head, and slow head led to slow, mind-blowing sex. He was in for a long night. But he had to interrupt her, because once she started, he wouldn't want her to stop. He pulled away again and gazed into Dixyn's eyes. Bryce felt like he had run through what he wanted to say a million times. Yet right now, at the moment of truth, his words seemed to escape him. He had to say something, so he did the only thing he could do: speak from the heart. "I have something for you," he managed to say. Bryce pulled out the black box and revealed a three-carat, three-stone trilogy diamond engagement ring.

Dixyn's eyes began to water and she covered her mouth with her hands. She had waited for this day forever, and was beginning to believe it would never come.

Tears filled her eyes but no words flowed from her lips as she waited for Bryce to speak.

Dixyn's reaction caused a tear to well in the corner of Bryce's eye as well, but he quickly blinked to prevent it from falling. Where he was from, men showed little emotion and tears were a sign of weakness. Bryce was many things, but weak wasn't one of them.

"I want you in my life . . . for life," he announced, "in holy matrimony, for better or for worse." Bryce removed the stunning platinum ring from the box and reached for her left hand. He pointed to the two stones and diamond in the middle. "This represents our future . . ."

Tears began to flow freely from Dixyn's eyes; still she didn't utter a word.

He pointed to the two smaller stones on the side. "These represent our past and present . . . our life." He placed the immense ring on her finger. "Be mine for life; marry me. Hold me down forever as my wife." Although this wasn't quite the eloquent speech that Bryce had prepared in his mind, it would do—heartfelt, short, and to the point.

Dixyn's tears flowed uncontrollably now, and it seemed like an eternity before she was able to whisper, "Yes." Then she screamed, "Yes, yes, yes!" She admired her ring from afar and then up close. It was beautiful. Bryce chose perfectly; it was exactly what she wanted. He knew her too well. "Yes, Bryce, I will be your wife. I'll hold you down forever, no doubt, baby." She kissed him passionately and led him to the bed. Dixyn was immediately overcome by a heightened state of emotional bliss. She began aggressively tearing his clothes off; their desire could be suppressed no longer.

Bryce's heart beat wildly in anticipation of what was to come. Pure desperation drove him to quickly remove all remaining clothing.

Dixyn gently grabbed a handful of his rock-hard manhood, fondling it before dropping to her knees. She immediately opened her mouth and lovingly licked his dick, running her tongue from the tip to the base. Dixyn's pace was slow and deliberate as she tasted every inch of his love. As soon as she had enough of teasing Bryce, she took his shaft inside her warm, alluring mouth. Bryce knew exactly what was coming next. Dixyn gripped his dick with both hands and began bobbing her head wildly as she moved her hands in opposite directions. This was Dixyn's signature move. It was something that drove Bryce wild. He grabbed her head as he feverishly began making love to her mouth.

Dixyn's head game was addictive. She could bring Bryce to orgasm in a matter of seconds; they both knew that. Tonight was like any other night and Bryce wasn't fighting the feeling. Soon his body began to emit the faint sounds of heavy breathing and moans, which were music to Dixyn's ears; it made her work even harder to please her man. Meanwhile, Bryce had fallen into a frenzy. He drove his dick in and out of Dixyn's mouth, accidentally causing her to gag a few times.

Suddenly the head of his dick began to swell and a strong surge of semen burst from the top, filling Dixyn's mouth. "Oh my god!" Bryce exclaimed. Dixyn swallowed the fluid effortlessly and kept on going. As hard as he tried, Bryce couldn't pry her off his dick. Dixyn incessantly attacked his member as if her life depended on it.

For her efforts, Dixyn was rewarded with a rock-hard penis in her mouth again. Even Bryce was amazed by her sexual prowess. She had never done anything like this before. He didn't know what had gotten into her, but he hoped that there was more where that came from. Fully erect, Bryce was now ready to be inside of Dixyn. He helped her to her feet and led her to the bed. Once there, he shoved her to the mattress.

Bryce knew just how Dixyn liked it: rough. At that moment, he wanted nothing more than to please his woman. Spreading her legs, Bryce placed her in the missionary position. Slowly he guided the head of his penis into her wet, warm vagina, filling her with every inch of his manhood. Bryce quickly skipped the loving preludes, the slow probing strokes, and began to pound the insides of Dixyn's pussy.

"Yes, harder, baby, right there, baby!" she yelled. "Please don't stop!" Dixyn was far from being a dead fuck. She began grinding her hips, meeting Bryce's every movement with one of her own. He was putting it down and Dixyn was throwing it back. A thin coat of sweat glistened on the couple's bodies as they worked each other ferociously.

Bryce switched positions, flipping Dixyn onto her stomach. From the back was Dixyn's favorite position. She arched the small of her back and poked out her ass in an effort to receive all of him. Bryce knew he was hitting her spot as soon as he entered her, as Dixyn's groans grew louder and louder. In a trance, Bryce suppressed the strong urge to come again.

"Damn, this feels so fucking good!" she cried out. The harder and faster Bryce went, the closer Dixyn came to having an orgasm. Her excitement grew with each thrust.

Fucking her hard from behind, Bryce could only watch as Dixyn's body began to freeze. Suddenly, Dixyn clenched her walls tightly around Bryce's dick, releasing her orgasm wave after wave. "Mmmmmmm," she purred.

Knowing that he had satisfied his woman, Bryce allowed himself to release over Dixyn's buttocks. Then he immediately collapsed. He rolled onto his back, reached over, and pulled Dixyn close to him. She placed her head on his chest as they both lay exhausted on the bed. The peaceful silence of sleep quickly replaced the heavy breathing.

The loud sounds coming from the home security system jolted Dixyn from her slumber. Still groggy, it took a few seconds for the noise to fully register. Then Dixyn heard loud footsteps ascending the stairs. Frightened, she did the only thing she could do: she desperately shook Bryce until he awoke.

"What?" he said, irritated. Bryce hated when his serene sleep was interrupted.

"Bryce, wake up! The alarm is going off and someone's coming up the stairs."

Before Bryce could respond, the cause of the security alert was at the closed bedroom door. Dixyn cringed and hid behind Bryce. In a split second, the door burst open. "DEA!" a deep voice shouted. "Put your hands where we can see 'em." Flashlight beams suddenly illuminated the room and two husky Caucasian men rushed in, followed by half a dozen other officers dressed in black army fatigues and bulletproof vests. Dixyn was yanked out of bed naked, flung to the floor, and handcuffed. Bryce received harsher treatment, as he was body-slammed down hard and handcuffed tightly.

"Bryce Winters?" the federal agent barked as he rolled Bryce over onto his back. Another agent came over with an eight-by-ten photograph and handed it to his superior. The first agent stared at the picture and then shone his flashlight down on his captive. "Yeah, it's him. Looks like we came at a bad time, huh, Bryce? Looks like you and the old lady was rolling around in the sack. Hope it was good, because that is the last piece of ass you're gonna get for the next twenty years. Unless you start liking boys." The room burst into laughter. "You have the right to remain silent. Anything you say can and will be used against you in a court of law. You have the right to speak with an attorney and have one present during questioning. If you cannot afford a lawyer, one will be appointed to you."

Dixyn lay handcuffed on the floor, confused, but Bryce knew exactly what this was about. He had committed a cardinal sin: selling large quantities of drugs to a customer who turned out to be a federal agent. Initially he'd had a funny feeling about the guy, but another well-trusted client had reassured him that the guy was "good money." This momentary lapse in judgment had now come back to haunt him.

CHAPTER TWO

Three months later

"Eight hundred bucks, take it or leave it, miss, but that's my final offer," the pawn shop owner said.

"But you told me on the phone you would give me fifteen hundred!" Dixyn fired back.

"Listen, I know what I said. But—and this is a big but—that was before I saw the merchandise. I thought it was one thing; it turned out to be another. You can never be too sure about these things, especially jewelry, until you see it," he calmly replied. "Now, as I said before, it's eight hundred. Take it or leave it."

A lot had changed in Dixyn's life since Bryce was arrested, though she felt lucky not to have been locked up along with him. Financially, things were going from bad to worse. Bryce's impending federal trial had already exhausted any money he had stashed on the streets. Dixyn's car had been repossessed by the dealer; the Range Rover would be taken too as soon as the repo caught up with her. The town house was in foreclosure. It seemed like every day the bills continued to mount. Her money woes were so troubling that Dixyn felt like she was losing her sanity.

She nervously fiddled with the engagement ring that her fiancé had given her. It was more than just a ring to her. There was no dollar amount that she could place on it. Yet on the other hand, it was one of the few remaining items of value that she had left. Dixyn was torn by her need to sell the ring in order to stay above water, and the romantic notion of keeping it and suffering in silence.

"I don't have all day, miss. What are we going to do here?" the pawn shop owner asked, interrupting her thoughts.

"Okay, I'll take it," Dixyn said regretfully, handing over her engagement ring.

Secretly, the man smiled. He knew he had gotten over big time on Dixyn. The resale value on that ring was a whole lot more than the measly sum he was paying out to her, but he didn't feel one ounce of remorse. He wasn't in the caring business, he was in the business of making money: buy low and sell high. It was business, never personal.

"Gimme a minute. I have to write up a ticket and give you a receipt. The terms and conditions, as far as payments go, will be on the back. I suggest you read them carefully. I'll be right back with your cash."

Given the depth of Dixyn's financial woes, this money wouldn't go far in helping her get back on her feet. As far as she was concerned, the money was already spent.

Dixyn planned on using the cash to take care of some of her basic necessities, like turning her electricity back on, and whatever remained she would use to buy gas and go grocery shopping.

Cash in hand, Dixyn exited the pawn shop, even more stressed out than when she had entered. She agonized for days over this. The engagement ring was the last piece of Bryce she had. Now it was gone. Dixyn knew she wouldn't dare bring herself to tell him what she had done. She was too ashamed. As she drove away, her mind ran wild with all kinds of thoughts about Bryce and her financial future.

But Dixyn was in self-preservation mode right now. While Bryce had his legal matters to deal with, she had her own day-to-day, real-life issues to address, like taking care of her daughter and keeping a roof over their heads. With her breadwinner gone, suddenly she had a different set of priorities, like surviving. Dixyn stared into the abyss of an uncertain future. With no education other than a high school diploma, her sources of income were limited at best. Dixyn knew some tough times lay ahead if she didn't do something, and fast.

Immediately after Bryce's arrest, his brother B-Dub called Dixyn up and said he was going to hold her down financially. But as of yet, that hadn't materialized. Dixyn had never even seen him before and hadn't heard a word from him since. Even Kendra had warned her about this mythical dark knight who was supposed to ride into town and save the day.

"Bitch, you better stop waiting on some nigga you

don't know to help you. You better get up, get out, and get something on your own. A nigga got you into this predicament in the first place. D, save ya'self. You are the solution to all your problems. You wait on that nigga if you want. Just don't hold your breath. I been tryin' to tell you how to get this money, but your uppity ass won't listen to me."

Dixyn had to admit that Kendra had some valid points. Kendra was a hustler; she and Dixyn weren't of the same ilk. Kendra was a go-getter while Dixyn was used to having everything handed to her. As long as she'd known Kendra, she always had her own shit. *Fuck niggas, get money* was Kendra's mantra. Unfortunately for her, it was an attitude that got her in trouble from time to time. And now, with Bryce gone, Kendra was beginning to heavily influence Dixyn.

After running some errands and paying the electric company, Dixyn returned home to find the lights back on. As she put away her groceries, Dixyn briefly contemplated bringing her daughter back home. She felt like she couldn't take another day alone in the quiet house. Dixyn's mother had been watching the child on the night of her birthday—the morning after her home had been raided, she had asked her mother to keep the child while she dealt with the mess. But the months were passing.

Dixyn pushed the thought of reuniting with her child out of her mind. In this state, she would be unable to properly care for her daughter. Besides that, with no cable TV, no access to the Cartoon Network or Nickelodeon, Dixyn would be hard-pressed to entertain her.

Cable TV and the Internet used to be necessities, but they had suddenly turned into luxuries that she couldn't afford. Now Kendra crossed her mind again, so she picked up her cell phone.

"Well, it's about fuckin' time! You were supposed to have been called me back, bitch!" Kendra snapped on the other end of the line. "What's poppin'? Where you been?"

"Pawn shop," Dixyn mumbled.

"Bitch, speak up! I ain't understand a word you said."

"I said I was at the pawn shop," Dixyn repeated as her eyes began to water.

"Doin' what?"

"Kendra, don't play dumb. I finally did what I told you I was thinkin' about doin'." Dixyn shook her head, reliving the painful memory.

"Oooooohhhhh! How much you get?

"Eight hundred," Dixyn spat.

"Daaaaammmmmmnnnn! That's all?"

"Yup."

"You lyin'!"

"Kendra, why would I lie? That's all I got."

"Girlfriend, you got more than eight hundred funky-ass dollars," Kendra said. "You also got played. Ain't no fuckin' way in the world you let them muthafuckas at the pawn shop lowball you like that. You should have known better than to go for that."

One thing Dixyn didn't like about Kendra was that she was sometimes quick to criticize and she didn't always take time to listen, let alone sympathize. But regardless, like it or not, Kendra kept it real. Dixyn could have called someone else to hear what she wanted to hear, but Kendra always said what she thought.

Dixyn snapped, "Well maybe if you would have come like you said you would, then it wouldn't have gone down like that. Shit, what the fuck I know about pawning something?"

"Bitch, don't be mad at me 'cause I ain't go! I got problems of my own. I can't be holdin' ya hand every minute of the day. Every goddamn day I let you cry on my shoulder. Ain't that enough? Anyway, what else did you take up there? I know Bryce had a lot of other shit worth something."

"No, he didn't. I thought I told you that already. When they raided the house, the feds grabbed all of Bryce's jewelry and about seventy thousand in cash that he had stashed."

Kendra let loose a whistle into the phone. "That's a lot of racks."

"Tell me about it!" Dixyn cracked. "A bitch like me could use some of that money right now. Did I tell you that the bank is foreclosing on the town house? I got the car dealer calling me every other day, saying that if I don't turn in the Range, the delinquent payments will negatively affect my credit . . ."

Dixyn launched into the host of financial troubles she was currently experiencing. She had never confided in Kendra as much as she did now. But she needed a confidante, and Kendra was there.

Kendra sat on the other in of the phone halfheartedly listening while watching a repeat episode of *Love & Hip Hop*. She had heard this sad song before. Quite frankly, Dixyn was beginning to sound like a broken record. Kendra knew exactly how to help Dixyn out of her predicament, but her friend was either too stubborn or too scared to take her up on the offer.

After about an hour of venting to Kendra, a realization set in for Dixyn. She had two choices: she could either keep crying and complaining, or she could do something. "Kendra, what's up with the club?" she suddenly asked. "I'm about ready to take you up on that offer."

"What?" Kendra called out. "You kiddin' me, right?"

"Nope."

"Dead ass?" Kendra asked.

"Yup. Whatever that means."

"I'm on my way over there right now," Kendra announced. "Bitch, we needs to talk. Shit just got real."

An hour later, Kendra pulled her red Mercedes Benz C-Class coupe into the driveway and honked the horn. Dixyn hurried to the window, peeking through the blinds before opening the door. Dixyn was glad she had showed up this time.

"Kendra!" Dixyn greeted happily, hugging her friend.

As Kendra sashayed inside the house, Dixyn couldn't help but notice how her butt bulged out of her low-rise True Religion jeans. "Damn, Kendra, is it me or is your ass getting bigger?"

"Anal sex," Kendra replied bluntly, playfully smacking her behind.

"What?"

"Anal sex," Kendra repeated. "It makes ya ass fatter. I been fuckin' wit' dis dude and that's all he likes to do."

"Better hope that nigga ain't gay."

"With a dick that big, it would be a shame. Besides, don't knock it till you try it," she joked.

"I hear that."

With Kendra leading the way, the duo walked through the house until they reached the kitchen. Kendra made herself at home, taking a seat at the kitchen table. "I bought you somethin'," she said as she rummaged around in her purse. "If I could only find it now. Damn, there it is."

Kendra removed a plastic bag of kush, a high-grade form of marijuana, and handed it to Dixyn, who put the weed to her nose and inhaled its aroma. The smile that adorned her face signaled her approval.

"Here, bitch," Kendra added, tossing her a blunt wrap from her bag. "You can't do nuttin' without this."

Dixyn caught the blunt wrap and busied herself rolling up the kush. Moments later, she was hungrily licking the blunt to seal it. She inhaled deeply while igniting the flame, then exhaled through her nose, releasing a huge cloud of smoke.

Meanwhile, Kendra calmly removed a dollar bill from her purse and unfolded it, exposing the white powdery substance. She carefully dug her pinky nail into the mound of cocaine and shoveled hit after hit into her nostrils, then looked up to find Dixyn staring at her in amazement.

"What, bitch? You act like you ain't never seen no-body sniff coke."

"Ah . . ." Dixyn began to say. "Nothing." She was surprised by Kendra's drug of choice. But she was even more surprised by her friend's lack of discretion. It was as if this was normal everyday shit for her.

"Anyway," Kendra said as she put away her drug, "this stripping shit is easy. All you gotta do is shake ya ass for some thirsty-ass niggas and you can get your money. Easy."

"Damn, Kendra, you make it sound so simple," Dixyn replied between tokes on her blunt.

"Because it is. This shit ain't rocket science. You don't need a degree in physics or even a GED. Bum bitches do it, old bitches do it, and ugly bitches do it. But only bad bitches like me and you get top dollar. Them other hos have to fight for the scraps."

For an hour, Kendra went on to break down the ins and outs of the strip game, making it sound easy, while Dixyn expressed her concerns and reservations. When enough drugs were consumed by both women, they had convinced each other that what Kendra was saying was the truth. Dixyn was completely sold on the idea of mak-ing fast cash. The notion of finding some financial stabil-ity seemed to have won her over.

Persuaded that Dixyn was actually down to strip, Kendra took her to a local sex shop and bought her a few outfits for the club. She told Dixyn that she would speak to the club owner, Notti, to make sure that every-thing was a go.

As they drove back home, the duo made small talk before Kendra issued a stern warning.

"Yo, Dixyn, lemme warn you about one thing. Don't fuck with none of them bitches at the club. They ain't your friend. I am, and them bitches is no good. Again, I strongly advise you not to fuck with them. And most of all, don't tell those bitches ya business. If you tell them bitches ya business, you won't have no business. Feel me?"

"I feel you," Dixyn replied faintly.

Kendra didn't elaborate, nor did Dixyn question her about this. One thing was for sure—even if Dixyn wasn't feeling this situation, she was in it now.

CHAPTER THREE

The locker room door opened and the stream of music seemed to follow Dixyn as she crossed the entrance that separated the patrons from strippers. The sour scent of body odor mixed with cheap perfume caught her attention. She wrinkled up her nose, cautiously inspecting each locker number, looking for the one assigned to her. Dixyn felt alone, and for good reason. Her strip club tour guide, Kendra, was once again missing in action. Visions of a paranoid Kendra in some seedy hotel, coked out of her skull, ran through her mind. Dixyn shook off the thought, infuriated by her friend's absence.

Finally she found her locker, which was in the middle of the room, between the bathroom and the exit. It was a heavily trafficked area. Dixyn stood in front of her locker fully clothed, just as stuck as she imagined Kendra was, while a dozen or so scantily clad and naked bodies orbited around her. Although Kendra had given her a pep talk the night before, it was obvious that this didn't help her now. Suddenly Dixyn was having second thoughts about this entire situation. Her conscience was consumed by a series of flashbacks of the scenes which had brought her to this moment in the first place. *Pull it together*, she told herself. *Do it for your daughter.*

"Yo, Dixyn!" a familiar voice called out. "What's Gucci?"

Dixyn let out a huge sigh of relief. She spotted Kendra strutting her way through the locker room, coming toward her. This was enough for Dixyn to quickly regain her bravery and focus. Kendra's presence went a long way toward calming her nerves.

"Damn, Kendra, where the fuck have you been? I only called you all night."

"There you go with that shit again," Kendra responded. "I been busy. I'm here now, that's all that matters."

"My bad, Kendra. I thought you'd keep your word this time and actually come somewhere with me."

"Bitch, you killin' me. Stop actin' like a big baby 'bout shit. It's not that serious. I'm not always there when you call, but I'm always on time. You heard that song before? Enough of the chitchat, we gotta get dressed. It's almost time for you to go on."

"Go on?" Dixyn repeated weakly.

"Yeah, you know, strip!" Kendra fired back. "That is what you're here for and what you will be paid to do."

Kendra began to strip out of her street clothes with Dixyn following suit right beside her. They stuffed their personal belongings inside their respective lockers, leaving nothing but the outfits they planned on wearing and small designer clutch purses lying on the bench beside them.

Kendra donned bright gold, metallic, nine-inch heels with a matching G-string that seemed to disappear between her ass cheeks. She chose to remain topless, exposing her firm, ripe titties to anyone who looked her way. Dixyn was still getting dressed while Kendra stood anxiously waiting on her.

"You're after Fonda, girl. You ready?"

Dixyn untied the string from the bikini top around her neck, going topless like Kendra. She shrugged. "I guess so."

"Well, what is it going to take for you to be sure? You need a drink? You want me to get an E, a molly, or what?"

Kendra removed her MAC lipstick from her purse and applied a coat to her full lips. She pressed them together and smiled. "I know, do a line with me, then you'll be ready."

"You know I don't get down like that, Kendra." Dixyn walked over to the bathroom with Kendra close behind and looked into the mirror, adjusting her long false eyelashes. "Just break the money down to me again."

Kendra stood behind her and gently massaged her shoulders with her sweaty hands. She stared at her reflection as she spoke. "Notti charges all the boys at the door—that's the 'house.' We each get a part of that off the top. What we make on the floor is ours to keep. The harder you work, the more customers you get, the more money you get. You feel me, Dix?"

"Yeah."

"VIP is two fifty guaranteed, but it's up to you to go that route. Niggas are gonna press you, but you don't have to do anything you don't want to do. Remember that."

Dixyn had to admit that Kendra talked a good game. She told Dixyn she was perfect for the job. She promised all she had to do was look cute, shake her ass a little, and she would make more in one night than she would in a week working the average nine-to-five.

"Here comes Fonda," Kendra said abruptly. "That's the chick I told you about."

Fonda walked into the bathroom talking loudly. "I need a fuckin' drink! Those niggas are animals!"

Dixyn stared at the young woman's slender naked body while she checked herself out in the mirror. To Dixyn, she was entirely too pretty to be dancing for dollars. She looked like she should be in someone's hip-hop magazine. She was tall with beautiful long hair and perfect skin—though Fonda was far from the woman she appeared. She was right where she wanted to be, doing what she wanted to do. Fonda's money was long, and she surely put in the work for it.

"I have two VIPs lined up already. Rent is due, bitches!" Fonda tapped Dixyn on the shoulder and she jumped. "Yo, you Dixyn?"

"Yeah."

"Nice to meet you," Fonda said politely. "Now that the formalities are out of the way, you need a stage name. You look like a Destiny. Now, Notti said to hurry your ass

I
N
F
A
M
O
U
S

up. You're supposed to walk out as soon as I'm done."

"You sure you don't want any of this?" Kendra asked, holding out a few odd-looking pills in the palm of her hand.

"No, I'm good," Dixyn answered, standing up and adjusting the tiny thong.

Kendra slapped her hard on the ass. She and Fonda giggled. "Shake what your mama gave you, bitch."

What Dixyn's mother had given her was good sense and morals, but all of that had gone out the window when she started fucking around with Bryce Winters. Bryce Winters was well known because he moved units—major units. Before Bryce Winters, Dixyn Greene didn't even know what a "unit" was. It felt like Kendra was finishing the job that Bryce had started, corrupting her further.

As Dixyn began to make her way toward the door, she turned, expecting Kendra to be right there behind her. Instead, her friend had moved to the bathroom, drinking and drugging with Fonda.

"Go ahead, I'll be right there," Kendra promised.

Dixyn didn't even bother to reply. It was all or nothing now. Kendra had led the horse to water; all she had to do was drink. This was a surreal moment. Dixyn couldn't believe she was actually about to remove her clothes for money. She took one deep breath and opened the door, entering the club.

"Don't stop, pop that, don't stop . . ." Rapper French Montana's hit record was blaring through the sound system as Dixyn walked obediently to the stage. Her presence immediately caught the eyes of many patrons. Their lustful

stares inspected every part of her body. The looks were so long and so hard that Dixyn felt violated. Quickly she made her way through the crowd toward the stage. She found the area crowded with another large group of men. Dixyn navigated her way through them, but not without having her private parts groped by numerous customers.

The makeshift stage was elevated only a few feet off the floor with two poles that extended from floor to ceiling. Dixyn was literally within arm's reach of any horny man who wanted to touch her. She began to feel more nervous, and not just because of the rowdy men. It was the presence of the poles that truly rattled her. Kendra had neglected to mention them.

Dixyn surveyed her surroundings and didn't see anyone she recognized, so she took another deep breath, smiled, and walked to center stage. Dancing was the easy part; it was the possibility of getting recognized by someone she knew that scared her to death. While the bass pumped through Dixyn's body, she remembered what Kendra had told her. *Just pretend you're alone in your bedroom dancing for Bryce or twerkin' on his dick. You know how to ride dick, right?*

Dixyn bypassed the pole and decided to do exactly what Kendra suggested. She pretended she was in front of Bryce. She played with her titties just like he did. She dropped to the floor and loosened the string on the sides of her thong. She let it fall to the floor and grinded hard, just like she did when she rode Bryce. Dixyn turned around and caught a glimpse of a few full erections. The cheers and catcalls alerted her that it was time to show the goods.

Stripping was an out-of-body experience for Dixyn. She wound her hips to the ground, lay on her back, and opened her long legs wide. She licked her fingers and touched her spot, exactly the way Bryce did it. The crowd, which was already sexually charged and ready to fuck, went wild. They showered Dixyn with bills of all denominations, making it rain in the club. The sight of the money made her go at it even harder. She licked her lips and twerked around all angles of the stage. She rose to her feet and made her way to one of the poles, gyrated against it slowly, and shook her ass like a professional. Hands and hard dicks were everywhere, grabbing for her ass and trying to touch her pussy, although Kendra had promised there would be little to no physical contact. But with a bunch of hood niggas wanting to fuck something and only one chick on stage, it was hard to control. Finally, the bouncers descended on the stage in an attempt to keep the order. The crowd was forcibly kept at bay. Dixyn was free to concentrate back on what remained of her stage show instead of fretting over her own safety.

All the bills that cluttered the stage floor brought a smile to her face. Dixyn needed every penny of this money, and now it was hers for the taking. As the music faded, signaling the end of her set, Dixyn got on all fours and began stuffing the money—*her* money—in her clutch bag. What money she couldn't carry in her bag, Dixyn balled up in her hand, clinging to it for dear life, while she carefully walked off the stage. Now the only thing that really worried her was falling in the heels Kendra bought her the night before. As Dixyn made her way back toward the locker room, she was sexually propositioned more times than she could remember. She just smiled and kept it moving. All she wanted to do was get back to the locker room so she could count up her stash. As soon as Dixyn opened the door, Kendra met her and slapped her on her ass.

"See, bitch, I told you it was easy. You looked like you knew what the fuck you were doing out there. Made me proud, bitch."

"I was scared as fuck," Dixyn said. "Where were you?"

Kendra ignored her question. "You did good though. Now let's see how you handle ya'self in the VIP."

"Aw, hell no, Kendra, I'm not doing no VIP. I already told you that shit ain't for me. I got all the dough I need right here. This is enough."

"There's no such thing as enough," Kendra countered. "Think big, you'll get big."

Dixyn began to straighten out her bills. Kendra quickly exited the locker room, leaving Dixyn to silently count up a little over three hundred dollars. Then suddenly Kendra reappeared, interrupting her.

"I have a business proposition for you, Dix."

"I'm not doing VIP, Kendra," she repeated. "You need to go find someone else for that."

"It's better than that. All this dude wants is time. He just wanna kick it wit' you. Just you and him. This is legit. Straight up. No funny business."

"I'm not for sale, Kendra," Dixyn declared.

"He just wants to spend time, Dix. He's willing to pay for it. You should at least go see what he wants before you shut him down."

"Who is this guy who's willing to pay for 'time'?"

Kendra guaranteed, "He's legit."

"Send someone else," Dixyn insisted.

"He wants *you*," Kendra fired back.

"Let him want someone else."

"Dixyn, ain't you the same bitch that the bank is foreclosing on her town house? And ain't you the same bitch who didn't have lights on in the crib up until a few days ago? And ain't you—"

"I see your point, Kendra!" Dixyn yelled out.

"Good! I had to remind you 'cause I thought you forgot. Now lemme go line this nigga up for you."

"Is this dude really willing to pay for time? Don't bullshit me! Don't have me go up there thinking it's one thing and he's expecting something totally different."

Kendra leaned down and whispered in Dixyn's ear, "You're in no position to turn down any money."

"Okay, I'll meet the nigga. Just give me a few minutes to clear my head."

When Dixyn reemerged from the locker room, she could have sworn she was in the wrong club. There was gratuitous sex happening all around her, everywhere she looked. It resembled a wild orgy. What Dixyn didn't know was that she had stepped in the midst of a locked-door sexual smorgasbord for strippers that the club owner

Notti threw monthly. Not every dancer in the club participated, but the real moneymakers did. They chose to stay and sell their services under the guise of VIP and lap dances. Compensation came in many ways—drugs, cash, or both. If a dancer was really on her job, she could walk out of one of Notti's locked-door events with a few stacks easy.

Dixyn maneuvered through the club, utterly astounded by what she was witnessing. She hoped that patrons who weren't having sex were too preoccupied with getting drunk or getting high to notice her. She was grateful that she had slipped into street clothes. As soon as the secret rendezvous with the unknown client was over, she promised herself she was leaving.

Dixyn moved swiftly through the mobs of men who started reaching for her arms and smacking her on the ass. She spotted Kendra without even trying. Pausing momentarily, Dixyn witnessed her friend sitting in the corner next to some dude with her head buried in his lap, bobbing up and down. Dixyn moved on carefully, trying not to draw any attention. As she made her way to the stairs that led to the VIP area, she literally ran into Fonda.

"Dix!" Fonda shouted.

Dixyn smiled as they passed on the steps.

"Go get that money, girl. That nigga is waitin' for you in room two," Fonda told her.

Heading up the steps, Dixyn's mind began to race. Who was this dude who wanted to buy some time with her? The closer she got to the top of the stairs, the faster her heart began to beat. Dixyn reached the upper level, unsure of which way to go. She followed a trail of doors to her left and counted down the numbers until she reached room two.

Dixyn knocked softly on the door, hoping no one would respond.

"Come in," a deep voice said.

Dixyn turned the doorknob and cautiously entered the dimly lit room. The first object that caught her eye was a stack of money that lay neatly on the table alongside of a bottle of champagne placed in a bucket of ice.

"Don't be afraid. Ain't nobody in this room gonna hurt you."

There was something about the dude's voice that was reassuring. He didn't sound like a rapist or a pervert to Dixyn. She pushed the door open all the way, revealing a dark-skinned black male fashionably dressed in a blue denim True Religion outfit with matching blue and black Nike Foamposite sneakers. He had an oversized snapback New York Yankees hat pulled over his eyes.

"Sure took you long enough, Dix," he chided.

She stood silently in the doorway, unsure of what to say.

"Dixyn Greene!" he spat. "Stop playin' wit' me! Come in and close the door."

Now the stranger had her undivided attention. She entered the room for no other reason than to ascertain how this dude knew her government name. She closed the door slowly behind her and stood near it in case she needed to make a quick escape.

"To what do I owe this pleasure?" Dixyn asked with sarcasm.

"Oh, you got jokes, huh, ma?" the man replied. "The pleasure is all mine, Dixyn. Since you're being funny, what is a nice girl like you doin' in a place like this?"

"None of your business!" she countered. "I'm not here to talk about my personal life. Or me, for that matter. Those things won't be topics of discussions. So, like I said before, it's none of your business."

"I beg to differ, sweetheart. It *is* my business. You probably don't know me, but you know *of* me . . ."

Dixyn desperately tried to study the man's physical features, yet she couldn't quite see below the baseball cap.

"You probably know a certain member of my family better than me," he confessed. "Like my brother Bryce. Small world, right?"

Dixyn's eyes widened and she clasped her hand over her mouth. "Brian?" she whispered lowly.

The man raised his chin so that his eyes were no longer shrouded. His gaze met Dixyn's head on and he removed the baseball cap. Dixyn had to admit the physical resemblance with Bryce was striking.

"Live in the flesh," he stated. "But you can call me B-Dub."

"Please don't tell Bryce you saw me dancin' at a strip club. He'd kill me!" Dixyn blurted out. She had been attracted to becoming a stripper by the vast amount of money Kendra promised she would make and by the notion that she could remain anonymous in this dark, seedy underworld. Ironically, her identity had been discovered her very first night on the job.

"Oh, I doubt that," B-Dub said calmly. "I hate to say it, but my big bro's about to get an asshole full of time. He won't be killin' nobody anytime soon. C'mere, Dixyn, have a seat while we figure out what to do about this unfortunate incident. I'm sure we can work somethin' out. But of course, that's up to you."

Dixyn was too upset to comprehend everything B-Dub was saying. She sat down in the only other chair in the room and began to cry.

"Damn, Dixyn, you looked so fuckin' sexy and shit while you was up on that stage," he continued. "Every nigga in da club wanted a piece of that, ma. Including me. If you were mine, you wouldn't . . ."

B-Dub's conversation was going off track and he began hurling sexual innuendoes at Dixyn. She tried to shrug off the comments until it became clear that he was dead serious.

He reached out and ran his palm up Dixyn's leg, startling her. She quickly brushed his hand away. "What do you want from me?"

B-Dub looked at her and laughed. Then there was an awkward silence. "What do you think I want?" he finally replied. B-Dub let this hang in the air for what seemed to be an eternity before answering his own question: "YOU!"

CHAPTER FOUR

arly the next morning, Dixyn's doorbell sounded loudly several times. She wasn't expecting any company and assumed it was Kendra, or perhaps the FedEx or UPS man delivering a package. After all, she rarely had visitors to her home, even before Bryce got arrested. In her second-floor bedroom, Dixyn peeked from behind the curtain.

"Shit!" she exclaimed as soon as she laid eyes on B-Dub. She remained frozen behind the curtain watching him. She was unsure of what action to take, whether she should answer the door or act as if she wasn't home. She stood there silently, weighing her options.

"Dixyn, open up! I know you're in there!" he called out.

B-Dub's yelling was all the motivation Dixyn needed—these things didn't happen in this neighborhood. People in the community were quiet and they kept to themselves. B-Dub could cause a lot of unwanted commotion, which might lead to complaints by neighbors. They already wanted Dixyn out after her town house got raided. She rushed downstairs to answer the door.

"B-Dub, why are you screamin' out my name? This is a nice neighborhood, it ain't that kinda party over here," she reprimanded as she opened the door. "What are you doin' here? And how do you know where I live?"

"Look, that's neither here nor there," he responded. "If you know what's good for you, you'll let me in."

Slowly, Dixyn stepped aside to allow him the space to enter. As soon as he passed her, she noticed it: a black briefcase. If it wasn't for his ever-present New York Yankees snap-back hat, blue Levi's, and construction Timberland boots, B-Dub might have been mistaken for a black businessman in corporate America.

Dixyn closed the door and followed B-Dub obediently. She couldn't take her eyes off the suitcase. Her mind began to wander. What was this impromptu visit all about? And exactly what did that briefcase contain? B-Dub strolled confidently to the living room as if he knew exactly where he was going, then headed straight for the bar in the corner. He quickly scanned the shelves, shaking his head in disgust. "What, no Henny?"

His choice of drink made Dixyn wonder if B-Dub's similarities to Bryce went deeper than a physical level. Was he just acting like Bryce? Was he just trying to be like him?

"Nope. All gone," Dixyn confirmed. "Bryce finished the last of it the night he got locked up." The fact that B-Dub wanted to consume alcohol at this time in the morning spoke volumes to her. B-Dub was either stressed out or he had a pretty bad drinking problem.

"Figures," he replied, turning to face Dixyn. "Yo, sit down, we gotta talk." B-Dub walked casually across the room, taking stocking of everything, from the hardwood floors and remaining items of expensive furniture to Dixyn herself.

She eyed B-Dub carefully as he approached, studying his body language. He was being even more cocky and arrogant than he had the night before. She didn't know what this was all about, but she was sure she'd find out.

Complying with his request, Dixyn took a seat on the end of the couch and crossed her legs like a lady. Her form-fitting skirt revealed her well-toned thighs and calves. B-Dub walked over to her and gently placed the briefcase on the floor between them before sitting down. He patted the briefcase as if it were a family pet.

"Listen," he began. "I need you to take this briefcase somewhere for me, fam."

"What's in it?"

"Nuttin'," he told her. "What's inside is none of ya concern. It's nuttin' illegal. Nobody's gonna get hurt. It's easy money, fam."

"Then you go!" she barked, staring at B-Dub, waiting for some sort of explanation. "I'm not tryin' to be in nobody's jail for some shit I know nothing about. Understand?"

"Oh, you gon' do me like that, fam?"

"Yup," Dixyn said.

"I *need* you to go. The girl who normally goes can't make it tonight. I know this is short notice, but you do kinda owe me a favor."

"Owe you?"

"Yeah, owe me. So you goin'. Like it or not."

"Really?" Dixyn shot back.

B-Dub immediately pulled out his iPhone and tapped the screen a few times. Then he handed it over Dixyn. "Go 'head, take a look at that, fam," he instructed her.

Dixyn swiped her finger across the touch screen and began scrolling through photos. Suddenly her eyes filled with tears and she covered her mouth in shock. "Why?" she whispered. "Why did you photograph me dancing? Who does this type of shit? You sick bastard. What are you tryin' to do to me?" She began erasing the photographs of her scantily clad body in compromising positions from his phone one by one.

B-Dub didn't even move a muscle—a fact that wasn't lost on Dixyn. In fact, his lack of movement disturbed her.

"I don't know what you think you're doin'," he said. "You can erase them off my phone, but I have them backed up elsewhere. How dumb do you think I am?"

Out of frustration, Dixyn threw the phone on the couch and glared at him.

With a sinister smirk on his face, B-Dub continued, "So like I was sayin' before I was so rudely interrupted . . . I NEED YOU TO DELIVER THIS BRIEFCASE FOR ME. You're gonna drive your car south to the Quantico marine base . . ."

Dixyn listened intently as B-Dub outlined the details of the trip. He told her exactly what she was to do and who she was to see. He told her this was "easy money" so many times that Dixyn began to believe him. If B-Dub had anything else in mind aside from having her deliver the briefcase, he did not divulge it.

"You the only person I can trust. We fam, baby," B-Dub explained.

Whenever he referred to her as *fam*, it made Dixyn cringe. It was unsettling the way he emphasized the word, giving it an entirely new meaning.

"You ain't no family of mine!" Dixyn fired back. "Family don't do me like this."

"Then consider me a friend, ma."

"B-Dub, or whatever you call yourself . . . we damn sure not friends. We not even friendly."

"Damn, Dixyn, those are such harsh words. But if I wasn't a friend, would I do this?" he asked, reaching into his pocket and retrieving a wad of money. "Here you go."

As bad as Dixyn needed the money, she was unmoved by B-Dub's sudden display of generosity. "That's nice," she said flatly, placing the money on the coffee table. For the short period of time she had known him, Dixyn had already seen that everything about this dude had a string attached to it.

B-Dub suddenly exploded: "You ungrateful ho! Don't be stupid. You better take that money. You was just sha-kin' ya ass like a li'l slut yesterday for some bread." The harsh tone of his voice put the fear of God in Dixyn. She didn't want a physical confrontation with him because it was one that she probably would not win.

He made a move to reclaim his money, but Dixyn beat him to it. She snatched it up and placed it in her bra for safe keeping. When she brought her hands down to rest on her lap, B-Dub reached over and massaged her empty ring finger. She quickly drew back her hand.

"Don't think I didn't notice that ya rock was gone. I noticed that from the moment I walked in here. It's a goddamn shame you had to get rid of it. But now that I'm around, you ain't gotta go through no more hard times or bad times . . . if you play your cards right."

Dixyn was stunned, but tried not to show it. *How the hell does he know what happened to the ring?* B-Dub seemed to know every little thing about her. She was beginning to think that running into him at the club had been more than just coincidence.

"My ring is upstairs!" Dixyn spat.

"Go get it. Make a liar out of me," B-Dub proclaimed.

"You know that I don't gotta prove nuttin' to you."

"You're right, you sure don't," he answered. "But I know who you do gotta answer to, and that's my dear brother Bryce. And I think it'll break his heart when I tell him that his so-called fiancée hocked his ring at the local pawn shop." B-Dub paused. "You know what, fam? We ain't even gotta take it there. See no evil, speak no evil, hear no evil. We'll keep that on the low. Only between us. Just do what I say and everything will go smooth. You feel me?"

At the moment, the only thing Dixyn could feel was

animosity building in her heart. She knew she was being blackmailed. But even still, she was naive enough to
believe that if she made this delivery for B-Dub, this one
time, she could be done with him.

Dixyn drove slowly down I-95 even though she was running late. She carefully obeyed the speed limit for two
reasons: First, she didn't want to take the chance of getting pulled over, especially when she didn't know what
was inside the briefcase she had in her car. The other
reason was that the extra time afforded her the chance to
gather her thoughts. She just wanted this night to be over
and done with already.

Just in case she got pulled over, she had rehearsed her
alibi: she was on her way to a family reunion in Richmond, Virginia. As far as Dixyn was concerned, this was
her story and she was sticking to it.

Secretly, she hoped that by arriving late, the person
she was showing up to meet would leave. Then there
would be no transaction to make. B-Dub would see that
she was a failure and never ask her to do something like
this again. Suddenly, so much was going on in her life;
the thoughts running through Dixyn's mind came fast.
She pictured what Bryce would say or do once he found
out what she had been up to lately. Then she thought
about what she was carrying and how much time it could
possibly get her if she was caught. As badly as Dixyn
wanted to turn around and go home, she knew she had
to at least show up, if only just to say she was there.

Quantico 5 miles, the sign read.

Dixyn carefully guided the Range Rover into the parking lot of a nondescript building housing a Chinese restaurant which looked like it had once been owned by some fast food burger chain. She could hear gravel being crushed beneath the car's tires, and a light cloud of dust trailed the SUV. Dixyn proceeded with caution, examining each car in the lot for passengers. She was anxious to make the drop and go on about her business.

B-Dub hadn't told her who to look for; he merely told her where to go, and when she got there, someone would contact her. After driving around the parking lot aimlessly for a few minutes, she noticed a car in the rear of the lot flash its high beams at her. Dixyn drove slowly toward the vehicle. The closer she got, the more apprehensive she became. Her HID headlights illuminated the inside of the car, allowing Dixyn to see its occupant—a dark-skinned black male, clean cut and alone.

Suddenly Dixyn's mind was infiltrated by terrible thoughts. *Suppose this is the police and the package I'm carrying contains drugs? Suppose this entire thing is a setup?* In a split second, she changed her mind. She decided not to stop for the stranger, even as she saw him exiting his vehicle and flag her down.

"Dixyn!" the man called out.

She mashed her foot on the brake pedal, bringing the car to an abrupt halt. Dixyn sat there dumbfounded, looking in her rearview mirror as the stranger began approaching her car. The closer he got, the clearer his physical features became. Dixyn could tell he was in the military by his upright posture, and his gait looked as if he were marching in some imaginary platoon. If that wasn't enough, his haircut was a dead giveaway. As badly as Dixyn wanted to pull away, she forced herself to stay. She had so much riding on this. She couldn't drive off, at least not now.

As he arrived at the car, Dixyn let down her window. "Get in," she said, keeping a close eye on him as he passed by the front of the vehicle, looking for something that would suggest the guy worked for law enforcement, like a pair of handcuffs, a concealed weapon, or a badge. She saw none.

"Didn't you see me flash my lights back there?" he asked politely as he slipped inside the car.

"No," Dixyn lied, straight-faced. She eased the car into an open parking space and killed the engine and the lights so as not to attract any attention.

"Okay," the man said brusquely, "where's the suitcase?"

Dixyn absentmindedly replied, "What?"

"The suitcase," the man sternly repeated. "You know, the object that B-Dub gave to you to bring to me."

"Oh yeah!" Dixyn exclaimed. "I'm sorry, my mind was somewhere else. I'll get it for you right now."

Dixyn exited the vehicle and retrieved the briefcase from the cargo area. When she returned to her seat, she handed over the item in question. The stranger set the briefcase gently on his lap and fetched a small key from his pants pocket. Then he paused momentarily.

"Do you mind if I open the briefcase?" he suddenly asked.

"No. Go right ahead." At this point, Dixyn's curiosity was getting the best of her. She was eager to see just what she had been transporting.

As the stranger successfully unlocked the briefcase, Dixyn just sat there beside him, stealing nervous glances at it. Slowly the top began to rise, and she peeked inside and saw nothing but money, neatly stacked in denominations of hundreds, fifties, and twenties. Dixyn couldn't believe her eyes.

Feeling her gaze upon the money, the man turned toward Dixyn and smiled. "I don't care what they say about B-Dub, he's all right with me." Quickly, the man closed the suitcase and locked it.

Dixyn shifted her gaze away, pretending not to be paying attention.

The stranger continued, "Could you pull up right next to my car?"

"Yeah," Dixyn answered, surprised.

The stranger climbed out and walked to the rear of his car. He opened his trunk, which obscured Dixyn's view of him. She didn't know what he was doing, but whatever it was, he was taking too long.

Suddenly the man reappeared carrying a large box with a lock on top. Dixyn watched the man struggle as he brought it over to her.

"Where you goin' with that?" she asked.

"B-Dub didn't tell you that you were also supposed to pick something up?"

"No, he didn't."

"Well, that's between you and him. After I put this

box in the back of your car, I could care less what you do with it. I fulfilled my end of the deal, okay?"

Dixyn didn't like the idea of being kept in the blind about delivering a return shipment to B-Dub. But like everything else on this job, she had little say in the matter. She opened the lift gate and watched as the stranger strained to lift the box inside. She felt the Range Rover lurch once the man finally heaved it in. *What the hell is inside that box?* she wondered. Yet she didn't want to give this too much thought because it only made her more paranoid.

"All right. You're good to go," the stranger said. "Drive safe. And I'll let B-Dub know you're on your way. Oh, and one more thing: one of your taillights is out. Looks like a bulb has blown. You might wanna get that taken care of ASAP."

"Okay. Thanks," Dixyn said flatly as she pulled out, leaving a cloud of dust in her wake.

Dixyn hit the highway, taking the same route back. Once again she drove cautiously, maintaining the speed limit. She watched enviously as cars sped past her but refused to throw caution to the wind. A few miles down the road, Dixyn felt vindicated when she saw a swirl of blue and red lights and a car on the shoulder that had been pulled over by the Virginia state troopers in an apparent speed trap.

"Better them than me," Dixyn mused aloud as she drove by.

The closer Dixyn got to her exit, the more she felt

at ease. Now all she thought about was collecting her payment from B-Dub and getting that box out of her car. Then Dixyn glanced in her rearview mirror and noticed a car tailing her a little too closely. She moved from the far right lane to the center lane, hoping the driver just wanted to pass. To her dismay, the car followed her into the center lane. Dixyn was beginning to worry once again. Suddenly her car was doused with bright red and blue flashing lights. Dixyn's heart sank to her stomach.

"Shit!" Dixyn cried out. "Why you pullin' me over? I wasn't even speeding."

With all the fear that was pinned up inside her body, Dixyn was overcome by the urge to floor it. But for her, escape wasn't a viable option. She knew one or two things would happen: either she would be caught by the police in a wild high-speed chase or she'd die a horrific death of blood and twisted metal. Neither option was appealing to her. Not getting herself arrested was a more pressing priority.

Dixyn pulled over to the side of the highway in a dark, desolate spot. The heavily tinted unmarked police car followed her closely. As she put her car in park and turned off the ignition, Dixyn nervously tried to get a glimpse of the officer in her rearview mirror. Unfortunately, she was blinded by the floodlight the officer had placed on her vehicle. So Dixyn simply sat back and waited for the officer to approach.

A knock on the window startled her, even though she knew it was coming. *Oh my God*, she thought, shying away from the window, holding her heart.

"License and registration, please," the state trooper said with a Southern twang.

"Excuse me, officer, what's the problem?" she asked while rolling down her window. "You can't possibly be pulling me over for speeding. I was doing the speed limit. My car was on cruise control and I—"

"Hold on for a minute, ma'am. I'll get to that. Right now, would you please produce your license and registration? Thank you."

As Dixyn began digging through her designer purse for the proper credentials, the trooper eyed the interior of the vehicle. All he needed was a reason, and any reason would do, to search the car. Finding both her Virginia driver's license and her registration, Dixyn handed them over without uttering another word.

"Gimme a minute, ma'am. I'll be right back," the trooper stated before returning to his unmarked car.

Dixyn wasn't worried about him finding any outstanding warrants on her, and she knew both her license and registration were valid. What worried her was the box in the back. She took a deep breath in an attempt to calm herself down. It seemed like it was taking an eternity for the cop to return to her car with her identification and an explanation.

Suddenly, out of nowhere, another state trooper's car pulled up. In the distance, Dixyn could hear the loud barking of a dog. Her heart began to beat rapidly. *This can't be happening.*

Not only had Dixyn been stopped by the state troopers, now they had called in the K-9 unit. She just knew she was going to jail. She was simply waiting to be placed under arrest. She didn't know what was in that box, but she was pretty sure that whatever it was, it wasn't legal.

The sounds of footsteps approaching snapped Dixyn back to reality. She looked in her mirror just in time to see shadows of state troopers on both sides of her vehicle. Dixyn took another deep breath and waited.

"Good evening, Ms. Greene. Sorry to hold you up, but the reason I stopped you was not because you were speeding or anything like that. It was because your driver's-side taillight is out."

Although Dixyn couldn't see the other cop, she suspected he was examining the inside of her car while she was being distracted by the conversation. That didn't really bother her. What did bother her was the dog that accompanied the other officer. She could hear it sniffing around as the state trooper barked commands. Dixyn prayed that the animal didn't go berserk and give the troopers a reason to search her car.

"You may not know this," the trooper at her window said, "but there has been a whole lot of drug smuggling up and down this very highway. Where did you say you were coming from, ma'am?"

Dixyn shot the trooper a look of disbelief, like she was offended by what he was trying to insinuate. Still, she chose her words carefully. "I didn't say, sir. But if you really must know, I'm coming from a family reunion in Richmond." Dixyn turned around and glanced at the other cop. Just as she'd imagined, he was snooping around, looking inside her car. "What's he doing back there?"

"Nothing out of the ordinary, ma'am. As I said, this corridor of I-95 has an unusual amount of drug trafficking due to its proximity to DC and Richmond."

Dixyn sucked her teeth. "So what does that have to do with me?"

"Well, I hate to say this, but you're driving this fancy car and it's not registered in your name—"

"Excuse me, officer, this is my fiancé's car!" she cut him off. "And just so you know, he's a veteran of the United States Army. He served two tours of duty in Iraq. He risked his life for this country. I think he is entitled to buy any kind of car he wants, as long as he can afford it."

"You're absolutely right," the man replied. "But you're missing my point. Would you mind if we searched the car? It'll only take a minute, and then you can be on your way."

Inwardly, Dixyn flinched at the thought. There was no way on God's green earth she could let that happen. Her mind raced with lies she could tell that would keep them at bay. Then she remembered something Bryce had once told her when they got pulled over in a so-called routine traffic stop. *If the police ever ask to search your car, always say no. If it was within their rights, then they would never ask you.*

"I don't have anything to hide," Dixyn snapped. "But no, you can't search my car. I know my rights, I'm not stupid. There's such thing as probable cause. You can't just violate my rights . . ."

Dixyn should have gotten an Academy Award for the angry black woman she was pretending to be. She hoped the mention of her civil liberties would be enough to scare off these overzealous state troopers.

"Take it easy, ma'am. No one's going to violate your rights. I just asked you a question. It was well within your right to say no. And you did."

Rising away from the driver's-side window, the state trooper motioned with his head to his backup to retreat. The two convened at the rear of Dixyn's vehicle, speaking in hushed tones. They conferred for a few moments before the trooper with the K-9 hurriedly exited the scene. Dixyn watched him speed off with his lights flashing. Obviously he had a more important call. She was finally able to breathe easy again.

The other state trooper returned to Dixyn's window. "Here you go, ma'am," he said, handing over her license and registration. "I'm gonna let you go with a warning this time. But do yourself a favor and get that bulb replaced. Have a nice night and get home safe."

"You too, officer."

Pulling back onto the highway, Dixyn said a silent prayer, thanking God for sparing her. She was free. Never in her life had this freedom meant more to her than right now.

CHAPTER FIVE

inishing up her breakfast, Dixyn kept glancing over at her phone to see if B-Dub had returned her calls from last night. She saw no texts or missed calls from him, but she did notice a text from Kendra.

What's good? I ain't heard from you since you made all that dough the other nite. Hope you putting that money to good use. Anyway call me later. I gotta holla atcha bout something. Don't call me too fucking early bitch. U know I'm not a morning person. LOL.

Dixyn chuckled to herself. Kendra wasn't lying about not being a morning person. She didn't wake up until late afternoon, early evening. If you knew Kendra, then surely you knew that much about her. But Dixyn was also curious what it was that Kendra had to holla at her about.

For now, she didn't entertain any more thoughts

about Kendra. She had other things on her mind—namely, B-Dub. She wanted him to come over to her house and get his shit ASAP. Dixyn had a full day ahead of her. She was going to run some errands, pay some bills, and then go see her daughter. Anxious to get her day started, Dixyn picked up the phone and dialed B-Dub again.

"Hello?" he answered.

"B-Dub," Dixyn said, thinking that his name sounded funny rolling off her tongue, "I been tryin' to reach you since last night. You didn't see all those missed calls from me? Huh?"

"Nope. My service is kinda bad in this area for some reason. Everything good?"

"It'll be even better once you pick up this package. Why you ain't tell me about that?"

"It musta slipped my mind, fam. But don't worry, I got a li'l extra somethin' somethin' for you."

"If you could come over here and get this I would greatly appreciate it. I got some things to do today and this be holdin' me up."

"A'ight, I'll be there."

"When?" she pressed.

"I'll be there," he repeated.

"B-Dub, can you please tell me when I can expect you? Like I said . . ." Dixyn's voice trailed off as she realized he was no longer on the line.

While she awaited B-Dub's arrival, Dixyn headed upstairs to take a shower, get dressed, and prepare for her day.

* * *

Beep! Beep!

The honk of a horn pulled Dixyn away from her favorite soap opera, *The Young and the Restless*. She raced to her living room window and saw **B-Dub** sitting arrogantly behind the wheel of a platinum Mercedes Benz S550.

Dixyn ran to the front door before he could blow the horn again. "Pull up into the garage!" she yelled.

Dixyn jogged through her town house to the entrance to the garage. She opened the door and hit a switch on the wall. Slowly the garage door began to rise, and as soon as there was enough clearance, B-Dub pulled in.

Dixyn hit the switch again and the door began to descend. Then she walked over to her Range Rover and opened the lift gate. B-Dub took his time exiting his car.

"Damn, Dixyn, every time I see you, fam, you lookin' betta and betta," he commented. "Lemme find out that you tryin' to seduce da kid."

"Knock it off, B-Dub. I ain't got no time for none of your shenanigans today. I'm already runnin' late, thanks to you. Oh, by the way, the cops pulled me over last night. I could've went to jail for whatever it is I'm transporting in my car."

B-Dub stood there with a callous look on his face. He seemed more interested in the box than Dixyn's story. "Well obviously you didn't or we wouldn't be here having this conversation," he declared. "Now would we?"

Dixyn stared at him coldly. "B, instead of bein' a wise-ass, you should be kissing *my* ass, thanking me for not getting locked up with your shit."

"Thanks," he said with a hint of sarcasm. "You did good." B-Dub reached in his pocket, removing a wad of money, and handed it to her.

Dixyn took the money without bothering to count it and slipped it in her pocket. "What the fuck is in that box?"

"If it makes you feel better, I'll open it and show you," he said while digging in his pocket for his keys.

B-Dub inserted a key into the lock and opened the box. Dixyn was infuriated by what she saw—guns, and lots of them. There were military-issued nine millimeters, .45-caliber handguns, and a few assault rifles.

She had been duped, but she was beginning to see right through B-Dub and his hidden agendas. "Just when I thought you could sink no lower, you turn around and do me dirty like this? What the fuck is on your mind, man?"

"Look, it was a last-minute thing," he proclaimed. "My connect wasn't sure if he would be able to get his hands on these bad boys. When he did, I couldn't turn 'em down. Do you realize how much money this shit is worth on the streets of New York?"

"No, I don't," Dixyn replied. "So what, you're a gun runner now?"

"Oh, my bad, ya used ta drug dealers like my brother. Well, I'm a hustler, but there's a difference, a very big difference, between the two. Drug dealers sell drugs. Hustlers sell everything. Even dreams."

"Ha ha! Very funny," Dixyn said. "Just grab ya guns and leave."

B-Dub ignored her completely, continuing to marvel at his cache of weapons.

Dixyn continued, "Excuse me. Excuse me . . ."

Without warning, B-Dub exploded into action. He rushed Dixyn so fast she had no time to react. Pressing her against the car, he slipped his hand inside her sweatpants and groped her vagina.

"Get the fuck off me, Brian!" she yelled. "You trippin' right now?"

Instead of releasing her, B-Dub leaned in closer and attempted to kiss her on the lips. Dixyn turned her head to avoid him.

B-Dub was losing control of himself. "Oh, you gonna do me like that, huh? You gon' make me take this pussy?" With one arm B-Dub pinned her to the Range Rover, and with his free hand, he grabbed a handful of her white T-shirt and bra and tugged on it with all his might. He damn near succeeded in ripping the clothing clean from her body. Strips of her bra and T-shirt dangled near her exposed breasts.

Now Dixyn was furious. In her mind, she had done nothing to deserve this. A new kind of rage surged through her body. What she lacked in strength and body weight she more than made up for in ferocity. She unleashed a knee to B-Dub's groin. Unfortunately for her, it didn't connect flush. Still, the blow was enough to back him up off of her.

Dixyn stayed on the attack, swinging wildly, and every blow she threw was launched with bad intentions. She really wanted to hurt him. But B-Dub wasn't exactly a slouch with his own hands. He weaved or blocked every blow that came close to landing. He even taunted Dixyn with laughter.

"Muthafucka, stop runnin' and fight like a man!" Dixyn called out.

B-Dub stayed his distance, waiting for her to tire herself out or let her emotions lead her into a crucial mistake.

Dixyn swung a wild looping right hand, and suddenly B-Dub closed in on her. "Uh-huh, I got ya ass now."

Once he slipped another wild left, B-Dub grabbed her arm and threw her to the floor. Landing on top of her, he used his body weight to smother her blows. When Dixyn began biting and scratching, B-Dub squirmed and wiggled to avoid serious damage, all the while grinding himself into her and roughly groping her breasts. Slowly he began to assert his total dominance over Dixyn.

Realizing that her best efforts were futile, Dixyn quickly changed strategies. A few months ago, she had seen a show on Lifetime about rapists and victims. She noted the fact that rapists get off on dominating others. If the victim stopped acting like a victim and instead like a willing participant, sometimes that was enough to thwart the attack. Armed with that knowledge, Dixyn decided to test out the theory. Immediately, she stopped struggling, becoming totally submissive. She began gently caressing his body as if she were enjoying what was going on. She wrapped her arms around B-Dub and pulled him closer, as if he were her lover.

"Damn, daddy, you gotta big dick," she told him. "Bryce ain't got nuttin' on you."

Dixyn could feel the sticky heat from B-Dub's breath on the side her neck. Just the thought of having sex with her fiancé's brother sickened her. She hoped like hell that this psychological ploy worked, because if not, she was going to get her ass whooped or end up giving up some pussy. There were no two ways about it.

"Take me upstairs and fuck da shit out of me," Dixyn begged him. "Let's go to the bedroom and I'll let you fuck me anywhere you want: my ass, my mouth . . . You can have me however you like . . ."

At first it was hard to tell if her words were having any effect on B-Dub at all. He continued his savagery, voraciously licking her neck, acting as if this was all fore-play. Dixyn had little choice but to up the ante.

She began kissing B-Dub passionately—long, deep, wet kisses. The move shocked him, yet he went right along with it. Somehow Dixyn managed to roll them both onto their sides. That created enough space for her to start fondling him. She unzipped his pants, removed his average-sized dick. Dixyn squeezed his manhood, and began jerking him off. Then she resumed talking dirty to him.

"C'mon, big man, fuck me," she insisted. "Let's take it in the house."

In the midst of the hand job, B-Dub peered at Dixyn with complete disdain. Instantly he began to lose his erection. Dixyn could feel his dick shriveling up in her hand. To save face, he broke away from her.

"Sorry," he said while getting to his feet. Then he straightened up his clothes. "My bad."

His apology baffled Dixyn. She didn't know what to make of the situation. All she knew was that whatever she had done or said worked. Considering what could have happened, she thought she had made out good.

B-Dub extended his hand in an offer to help her up. Thinking it was some type of trick, Dixyn refused it.

"I can get up by myself. I don't need ya help," she told him.

Finally Dixyn rose to her feet, and as if she was suddenly aware that her breasts were exposed, she crossed her arms over her chest.

"Yo, I'ma have to leave some of these guns here. I can't take 'em all, my trunk's not big enough," B-Dub said.

"That's not my problem!" Dixyn snapped. "I want all ya shit outta my house."

"Yo, c'mon, fam. Could you do me this favor? There's no way in the world I'll be able to fit . . ."

Besides being a pervert, Dixyn thought something was seriously wrong with this man. He was carrying on a conversation as if nothing had happened. "Once again, not my problem. In case you didn't notice, you're not exactly one of my favorite people at the moment. I'm goin' in the house to get myself together. When I come back downstairs, I don't wanna find you or your guns inside my garage." Having successfully silenced him, Dixyn backed away from B-Dub, who now busied himself unloading the weapons from her Range Rover to his car. She didn't turn her back on him until she was safely inside her home.

Before even cleaning herself up, Dixyn watched and waited from the inside until B-Dub had left. Once she was sure he was gone, she went upstairs to take a shower, the incident having left her feeling more than a little filthy. She felt morally unclean. Even the thought of kissing B-Dub repulsed her.

Inside the shower, the hot water cascaded down on Dixyn's body, relaxing her. She stood directly underneath the showerhead lost in thought. For the life of her, she couldn't understand B-Dub, nor was she really trying to. She couldn't believe the audacity of him trying to force himself on her! What was especially strange to her was that the person who was supposedly helping her out of a bad spot was the same person who now seemed to be ruining her life. In her fiancé's absence, Dixyn was being forced to rely on a man who clearly didn't have her best interests at heart.

CHAPTER SIX

What a life! Dixyn was thinking as she drove around running her errands. The things she had to do to get ahead were troubling her.

For the first time in a while, she was beginning to chip away at her mounting debt. With the money she had been making over the course of the past week, Dixyn caught up on the delinquent car note, deposited some money in the bank to stop the foreclosure, turned her cable back on, and took her car to a mechanic to have the rear brake bulb replaced. But she remained far from happy.

Dixyn felt that her life was incomplete. She felt alone in this world without the man she so desperately adored, and the love of her life, her daughter Ava. Realizing there was little she could do to remedy her fiancé's legal situation, her main goal was to finally bring her daughter back home.

It bothered Dixyn that she'd had to send her daughter to live with her mother. She wasn't the type to leave her daughter with anyone else, family member or not. In the past, Dixyn had routinely passed on girls' night out, dinner and drinks with some high school friends, especially if Bryce was out of town or handling some business and if her mother was unavailable. In her mind, Ava always came first.

But now things were different. In order to survive and maintain the luxuries that they had grown accustomed to, Dixyn had to sacrifice quality time with her daughter. This was a trade-off and she wasn't sure how long she could continue doing it. She hoped one day a change would come and things could go back to normal.

Dixyn tried to push these thoughts out of her mind. In a little while she would be holding her beloved Ava in her arms. That thought alone warmed her heart and brought a smile to her face.

A ring of her cell phone broke Dixyn's reverie. She hesitated before answering it, digging into her purse while keeping an eye on the road, hoping like hell it wasn't B-Dub. She was relieved when she saw Kendra's name on her phone's screen.

"What up, Ken?" she answered cheerfully.

"Damn, bitch, you can't call nobody?" Kendra fired back.

"My bad," Dixyn laughed. "I was kinda busy payin' these bills. I was gonna call you. But you beat me to it."

"Don't get brand new on me. Get a couple dollars and don't know how to act," Kendra said playfully. "Remember who ya true friends are."

"C'mon now, Kendra, stop playing. You know I don't get down like that."

"I know. I'm just fuckin' wit' you. Anyway, umm, I got a way for you to make some more money. You down?"

"Wait a minute, Kendra. I ain't gonna agree to nothing before I know exactly what I'm getting myself into."

"Okay, here's the deal. Some nigga from the club saw me dancin' and invited me to do a bachelor party for a friend of his. All you have to do is dance, nothing else if you don't want to. But of course if you suckin' and fuckin', you'll make more for yourself."

"I don't know, Kendra, you said the same thing last time," Dixyn responded. "And then you tried to sell me off to the highest bidder."

Kendra brushed the remark aside. "That was last time. This is different. It's a private party. Won't be a whole bunch of niggas tryin' to dig up in ya shit. These niggas got dough. They ain't pressed for pussy, they out to have a good time . . . "

Naturally, Dixyn had her reservations about this new situation. She was judging Kendra on her initial foray into the club, which hadn't been a good experience de-spite all the money she made. Still, she tried to keep an open mind and hear her out.

Kendra continued, "Besides that, I'm payin' you eight hundred dollars for one night's work. I'll give you half up front and the other half at the end of the night. Now how that sound?"

Dixyn wanted to say, *Too good to be true.* But she bit her

tongue, not wanting to start an argument. "All right, I'll do it," she said. "When is it?"

"Tomorrow night."

"Okay, so when do I get paid?" Dixyn asked.

"Bitch, that's all you worried about, huh? You money-hungry ho."

"If I am, I get it from you," Dixyn countered.

"I'll have that for you tonight. You workin' tonight, right?"

Dixyn didn't know how to respond. She'd been having mixed emotions about dancing at the club since that first day when B-Dub showed up. Considering her episode with him earlier that day, Dixyn was in no rush to come back in contact with him. She wanted to tell Kendra what had happened to her, but at the last minute decided against it. Kendra didn't have the most sympathetic ear.

"Y-y-yeah," Dixyn stammered. "I'll be there."

"Then I'll have that for you tonight," Kendra assured her. "Talk to you later. Gotta get my beauty sleep."

"Night-night," Dixyn replied. One thing she could say about Kendra: she was on top of her hustle. She always found a way to keep income flowing.

With her financial situation beginning to look more promising, and a little dough in her pockets , Dixyn felt it was time to pay that pawn shop a visit. She wanted her engagement ring back. At the next light, Dixyn took a sharp right and headed straight there.

She entered the store with an air of confidence that she hadn't possessed the last time she was there. She strolled past the well-arranged display cases of jewelry. Dixyn took note of how tidy the store was. The floors were cleaned, waxed, and buffed to a shine, and the merchandise in the aisle was neatly placed on individual shelves.

"Can I help you, ma'am?" one worker called out.

"No thanks. I see the gentleman I'm looking for right there," she said, pointing at a middle-aged Caucasian man.

Dixyn marched confidently over toward the glass counter where the guy stood and held out her pawn stub. "Remember me? I want my ring back," Dixyn declared. She placed her ticket on the counter along with her identification.

"Oh, yes," the man responded, pointing his finger back at Dixyn. "Greene? That's the name. Am I correct?"

"Yes, Dixyn Greene."

"Gimme a moment, please." He took the ticket and walked into the back of the store.

Dixyn turned her attention to the display case. She began eyeing the jewelry, wondering what the story was behind each item, why the owners pawned them off in the first place.

When the shop owner reappeared from the back, noticeably absent was Dixyn's engagement ring. Dixyn just stood there with her arms crossed.

"Where's my ring?" she blurted.

"Ms. Greene, I regret to inform you that your item has been sold."

"What the fuck you mean?" Dixyn exploded.

Without saying another word, the owner handed Dixyn her ticket. She was stunned.

"Sorry, ma'am. But if you like, I can show you some other comparable rings that you might be interested in."

His sales pitch further infuriated Dixyn. How dare he try to sell her a replacement ring at a time like this? She stomped out of the store, her mood severely altered. She couldn't believe her stroke of bad luck. How was she going to face Bryce without the engagement ring he had given her? What was he gonna say? As she mulled over the situation, she found she had more questions than answers. And the only thing Dixyn had in her possession at the moment was regret.

Dixyn flew down her mother's dirt road in Petersburg, Virginia. She had traveled this road so many times that she felt like she could do it with her eyes closed. There was no picturesque scenery here, nothing but dense trees and foliage. An occasional house dotted the landscape.

Dixyn remembered when she first took Bryce out here to meet her mother. He had said, "If I ever go on the run from the police, I'm coming out here. This is the middle of nowhere."

Off in the distance, she could see her mother's one-story ranch-style house slowly coming into view. She began to ease up off the accelerator. She didn't want anything like the squeal of her brakes or the rev of her engine to announce her presence. Dixyn wanted to surprise everyone, especially her daughter. Her trip to the country was a well-needed excursion from the fast lane she was currently moving in.

The Range Rover pulled to a slow, quiet stop in the driveway. Dixyn climbed out and closed the door softly. As she walked up the flower-lined driveway, she noticed Ava's pink Barbie 4x4 jeep that her father had bought her for Christmas. She remembered how her daughter had broken a lamp in the living room while learning how to operate the vehicle.

Dixyn used her spare key to open up the front door of her mother's house. The instant she crossed the threshold, her sense of smell was immediately awakened. Her mother was in the kitchen making one of Dixyn's favorite dishes, smothered pork chops with baked macaroni and cheese and collard greens with smoked pork neck bones. Quietly, Dixyn closed the front door and tiptoed through the house, following the rich aroma of the soul food. She peeked around the corner to the kitchen to see what was happening in there. Her mother was seasoning a pot of collard greens. Ava sat at the table her with her attention on the television screen. Dixyn didn't want to frighten her mother too badly, so she took out her phone and dialed the house phone.

"Hey, Dixyn," Mrs. Greene chimed. "I'm surprised to hear from you. You know, you could call this child of yours every so often—"

"Ma, I'm in the house."

"What you say?"

"I'm in the house, right around the corner from you." Dixyn stuck her head into the kitchen and waved to her mother. "Look over here. I didn't wanna scare the H-E-L-L outta you. But I wanted to surprise Ava. So hang up the phone and go back to cookin'. I wanna surprise Ava."

Crouched in a low position, Dixyn came out from hiding and tiptoed into the kitchen. Her mother glanced in her direction as she pretended to cook. Closer and closer, Dixyn inched up on Ava, and then she kneeled down when she was right upon her. Gently, she covered her daughter's eyes with her hands.

"Guess who?" Dixyn called out, trying to disguise her voice.

Ava made no attempt to move a muscle. An infectious smile spread across her face from ear to ear, and she began to giggle.

"Guess who, Ava?" Dixyn said again, this time returning to her normal voice.

Ava paused as if she were processing the vocal chords in her mind. "Mommy?" she answered unsurely.

When Dixyn removed her hands from her daughter's eyes, Ava whipped around in her chair, coming face to face with the woman who birthed her. "Mommy!" she shouted again.

Overcome by excitement, Dixyn scooped the girl up in her arms. She hugged her child tightly, as if her life depended on it. The joyous reunion bought a smile to Mrs. Greene's face.

"Hey, pretty girl, how has mama's baby been?" Dixyn pulled her daughter away from her body and planted wet kisses over her entire face. "I missed you so much. You know Mommy loves you." Dixyn wanted to say everything she was thinking to her daughter and at the same time say nothing at all. She marveled at how much Ava had grown since the last time she had seen her. The realization made her feel guilty.

"Mommy, Mommy, I love you too!" Ava cried out. "I was driving my car today. I helped Grandma cook. I'm a big girl now, Mommy."

"I can see that," Dixyn replied. She rose to her feet with her daughter attached to her thigh and admired the girl's physical features. It was uncanny how Ava had turned out to be the perfect blend of Dixyn and Bryce. She had her father's big brown eyes and wide smile. She had inherited Dixyn's small round nose as well as some of her mannerisms, such as moving her hands animatedly while talking. Even Ava's caramel complexion was a gorgeous mix of both parents, her father's dark skin and her mother's lighter tone.

"Who did your hair today, Ava?"

"Me, me, Mommy!" the girl exclaimed. "But Grandma helped me. Do you like my bows, Mommy?" Ava's sentences were becoming more refined and it took little effort to have a full conversation with her. Dixyn was amazed at how far she'd come in such a short time. Ava was only two and a half years old but had the vocabulary of a five- or six-year-old. Dixyn knew this was her mother's doing. Her child had benefited greatly from her short stay here.

"Of course I do!" Dixyn lied. "You look very pretty." She hated to see little girls with a million and one barrettes attached to heaps of ponytail braids. Dixyn had expressed her dislike for the hairstyle to her mother, but obviously the woman didn't listen or she just didn't care. Dixyn thought about bringing the matter to her mother's attention once again, but she resisted. This wasn't the time or the place for that. She realized some people would love to have her problem right now. Some people didn't have an adoring mother who took great care of a granddaughter at a moment's notice.

Instead, Dixyn walked over to her mother and leaned forward as if she was about to whisper a secret. "Mom, I love you. Thanks for taking care of my daughter. Thanks for everything."

"You're welcome, baby," her mother responded, dotting her daughter's cheek with kisses. "You're welcome." Love flowed through the room as the two women embraced.

"Mom, it's smelling so good up in here! You must have been reading my mind. I'm starving," Dixyn said.

"You know you're welcome to stay for dinner. Girl, have you been eating? You look like you losing weight. I wanted to say that as soon as I laid eyes on you."

"I eat, just not that much," Dixyn admitted. "I got other things on my mind besides stuffin' my face."

"Still, that's no reason to not to eat. Matthew 6:11 tells us, *Give us this day our daily bread . . .*"

Dixyn didn't need a sermon right now, especially with all the sin she had been committing lately. She was sorry she'd gotten her mother started. On many occasions, her mother had run her out of the house, preaching the word. Dixyn didn't want to this to be another one of those times, so she tried to change the subject: "Ma, where my stepdad at?"

Mrs. Greene was the talkative type and was easily lured by this. "He went fishing with his friend Earl," she replied. "He should be back sometime soon. So just stick around, he'd love to see you."

"I will. Now, Ma, can you please feed me?"

"Yes, baby. You and Ava go have a seat in the dining room and dinner will be served."

Dixyn bent down and scooped her daughter up in her arms before walking off to the dining room.

Her mother called out, "Girl, put that baby down. She can walk, run, turn cartwheels, and do everything else. You gon' spoil that baby. The Bible says, *Train up a child in a way he should go, and when he is older he shall not depart from it . . .*"

Dixyn laughed, her daughter clinging tightly to her body. She cherished moments like these, because she knew there would come a time when her daughter wouldn't want to be held. Until then, Dixyn planned on taking advantage of every opportunity.

Over dinner, the two women discussed things that were going on in Dixyn's and Ava's respective lives. While her mother was open and forthcoming, Dixyn had to be deceitful about everything, from what she was doing and where she was working to Bryce's legal situation. Although she hated to lie to her mother, she knew that there were certain things in this world the woman wouldn't understand, namely the streets. Her deeply religious roots wouldn't allow her to fathom certain situations.

Dixyn fabricated a story about working two jobs, one as a secretary for a prestigious law firm in DC and another as a weekend waitress at the local Waffle House. Her latest occupation was something she didn't care to share with the rest of the world.

Her mother believed the fiction wholeheartedly. She told Dixyn stories about Ava, all the progress she was making with the milestones in her life. Dixyn smiled outwardly, but inwardly she fought back tears. Silently, she promised herself that as soon as she was able to keep her head above water, she would bring Ava home. Dixyn prayed that it wouldn't be much longer.

A packed club greeted Dixyn the night she returned to work. She spoke briefly to the bouncers as she entered and her eyes scoured the place for any signs of Kendra. She was the main reason Dixyn had even come there. Dixyn zeroed in on her prancing around seminude. Making her way through the crowd, Dixyn followed her friend into the locker room.

"Kendra?" Dixyn called out.

When no answer came, she walked around the locker room in search of her friend. Dixyn expected to find her at her locker, but she wasn't there. She then headed over to the bathroom, where she heard loud sniffling sounds. She immediately knew it was Kendra and she also knew just what she was up to: sniffing cocaine in the toilet stall.

"Kendra?" Dixyn called out again.

"Yeah, gimme a second, I'll be right there, Dixyn!" Kendra shouted back.

Dixyn folded her arms, leaned up against the wall, and waited for her friend to finish getting high. From where she stood, she could see there were two pairs of legs in the stall. She was willing to bet that the other person was Fonda.

The toilet flushed, signaling that the get-high session was officially over and the ladies had hidden the contraband. The stall door opened and out walked Kendra, with Fonda following closely behind.

"Dix, what's Gucci?" Fonda greeted her.

Dixyn tried not to stare at their noses, but couldn't help herself. She glimpsed traces of cocaine around both of their nostrils. It surprised her how good Fonda was at disguising her high.

"I'm all right," Dixyn replied. "And ya'self?"

"You know me—another day, another dollar," Fonda cracked. "I heard you gonna do that bachelor party wit' us tomorrow night."

Dixyn just smiled and shook her head without saying anything. She noticed Kendra was being unusually quiet. Dixyn looked into her eyes and saw a blank crystal stare. *Must be the coke*, she mused. Kendra was falling deep into the evils of drugs and fast living. It was like each time Dixyn saw her in the club, Kendra was acting weirder and weirder. Her friend was slowly becoming damaged goods.

"Notti wants to see you," Kendra announced robotically.

"'Bout what?" Dixyn asked.

"How the fuck I'm supposed to know?" Kendra mouthed off. "He didn't tell me and I didn't ask."

"All right, lemme go see what this nigga wants before I put my bag down and get dressed," Dixyn said, exiting the bathroom.

"Dixyn, I got ya money as soon as you get back too," Kendra called after her.

Notti requesting to see her made Dixyn feel like she was back in high school on her way to the principal's office over some unknown violation. Since she'd started dancing at the club, she'd had little to no contact with the owner. In fact, Dixyn would be surprised if Notti even remembered her stage name.

His office was located right above the club, giving him a bird's-eye view of the entire joint. Slowly, Dixyn made her way up the dimly lit steps. When she reached the top, she saw a bright light coming from beneath the door all the way down the hall. She could faintly hear voices; the closer she got, the louder they became. When she reached the door she was unsure of what do, whether she should just enter or wait it out. Then the sound of a certain voice pricked her ear. It was B-Dub; she knew that New York accent anywhere. *What is he doing here?* she wondered.

Since the last incident, Dixyn hadn't gotten a call or text from B-Dub. She hoped he had disappeared for good, just as quickly as he entered her life. Now she could hear Notti discussing B-Dub's less-than-legal activities in the club.

". . . B, I hope I don't sound ungrateful, unapprecia-tive, or anything like that. But you gotta stop pushin' ya stuff in this joint, dog. I got word from a friend of mine in the sheriff's department that they supposed to be doin' a big bust soon. You know this is my place of business. This is how I eat. I'm not a jack-of-all-trades like you, or a hustler. I'm a businessman. I sell my patrons the idea of havin' a good time. Drug dealin' is bad for business—"

"Listen, you fat bastard!" B-Dub snapped. "You wasn't sayin' all that a couple months ago when ya rent was all backed up, when ya Atlantic City gambling habit had ya ass damn near in the poorhouse! My money was good then, but now all of a sudden it ain't good no more. I don't believe that shit you shovelin' 'bout some imagi-nary bust. Ya money got right, now all of a sudden you don't want a nigga round no more, fam . . ."

Dixyn had heard enough and quickly made her way back down the hallway, but the voices coming from the office grew louder.

"B, don't be like that. I paid you back your money and then some. But business is business. B, we're in two different occupations, from two different worlds."

"Yo, you just think ya gonna be able to do me like this? Me, the nigga who came to ya aid when no one else would?" B-Dub warned. "Fam, if you think you just gonna do me like that, you got anotha muthafuckin' thing comin' . . . Believe that!"

Dixyn found Kendra and collected half of her pay up front for the bachelor party the following night. She hid

out in the locker room to avoid both Notti and B-Dub.
After twenty minutes or so, she slid out of the club unde-
tected, preferring to spend the night alone at home over
dancing for dollars.

CHAPTER SEVEN

Before Dixyn arrived at the Henrico County Regional Jail, she already had a preconceived notion of how it would look. Boy, was she wrong! There were no twenty-foot fences with rows of razor-sharp barbwire adorning them, no prison guards armed with high-powered rifles ominously overlooking the grounds. Instead, what she found was a state-of-the-art burgundy-brown brick facility that looked almost like a college campus. Still, deep within the confines of the jail lay the love of her young life, Bryce Winters.

Dixyn entered the facility to register for her visit with her fiancé, and the first thing she noticed was how chilly it was in there. The climate-controlled room gave her goose bumps all over her body. The jail was immaculately clean from top to bottom, not a speck of dirt on the floor. Dixyn was surprised to see so few black visitors lined up to see their loved ones. What she did see was lots of poor white trash females who looked like they were fresh out of the trailer park. Most of these women's hair was undone and some were missing teeth. The dress code for the day must have been dirty denim blue jeans. Dixyn thought to herself, *I guess I didn't get the memo.* She almost felt out of place in her high heels, slacks, and short-sleeved blouse. Thank God the line wasn't too long, because Dixyn didn't think she could bear the sight of these woman much longer.

"First time here?" a woman asked her.

"Why?" Dixyn replied defensively.

"Because if it wasn't, you would have known to fill out the visitor registration form," the woman informed her.

"Well, where is it?"

"I have an extra one right here." The woman handed it to Dixyn.

"Thank you."

"Don't mention it. Just do as I do and you won't go wrong."

Dixyn ignored the comment, choosing not to engage any further in conversation with this stranger. As she filled out the registration form, she unconsciously began to stare at her ring finger. The absence of her engagement ring was enough to make her heart shatter all over again. She worried about what Bryce would say when he noticed. Her heart started pumping faster as she conjured lies to tell him.

"Who are you here to see, ma'am?" the corrections officer asked, looking up from his desk at the stunning black beauty before him.

"Bryce Winters," Dixyn replied.

The officer busied himself punching the inmate's name into the computer. Bryce had had a few scrapes with inmates and corrections officers alike since he'd been transferred from the Richmond county jail for his role in a brawl. Upon finding his information, the officer put in a call to his housing unit. "Bob, could you send inmate Bryce Winters down to the visiting room? He has someone here to see him."

Dixyn watched the corrections officer the entire time. She couldn't help but think how she could never do that job. Whether he admitted it or not, this guy was locked up for eight to sixteen hours a day, depending how long his shift was.

"I need to see your ID, ma'am."

"Oh, of course," Dixyn replied, producing her driver's license from her pants pocket.

The corrections officer quickly reviewed it and passed it back. "Ma'am, just follow the yellow line on the floor. It will lead you directly to the visiting room. And if that doesn't work, just follow the crowd. Unfortunately for some of our visitors, this isn't their first time here, if you know what I mean."

"Thank you." Dixyn smiled as she went on her way to see her fiancé.

Bryce sat in the visitor booth in a bright orange jumpsuit with the words *Henrico County Jail* emblazoned across his back. Clear, thick Plexiglas separated him from the outside world. He impatiently waited for his visitor to arrive.

Bryce thought it was either his private attorney or some-one from the federal prosecutor's office. Lately they had been offering a reduced sentence if he cooperated with their investigation. Bryce had flat-out refused to become a snitch for the government, even if it meant serving a lengthy sentence. His name and reputation meant more to him than getting out of prison a few years early.

Bryce busied himself looking at the other inmates' sisters, cousins, girlfriends, mothers, wives . . . any female who crossed his sight. Only a few of these women looked good enough for him to have sex with. Bryce blamed his rampant sexual urges on his four-month incarceration; he wouldn't give any of these broads the time of day if he were on the streets.

Jail was a far cry from the luxury Bryce had enjoyed a few months ago. Being imprisoned took a whole lot for him to get used to. He cursed out the corrections officers and fought with other inmates as he struggled with both the stress of his case and the everyday monotony of do-ing time. He had fought the institutional staff tooth and nail until slowly he came to the realization that he had to be here, so he might as well make his stay as pleasant as possible.

The sally port door opened, allowing Dixyn admit-tance into the visiting room. She was the very last person to enter, so it was easy to find her assigned seat—it was the only one still empty. As Dixyn walked along, her curves diverted inmate eyes to her body, which led to their sig-nificant others turning their heads to see just what their partners were looking at. Arguments soon erupted.

"Damn," one inmate moaned.

When Bryce finally saw what was causing this disturbance, he was shocked. This was not who he was expecting. The sight of Dixyn moving sensually toward his booth nearly stopped his heart. Yet his stoic expression stayed on his face. Dixyn beamed brightly at Bryce as she took her seat and picked up the phone. For a precious few moments, she couldn't speak as she peered at him through the thick glass. Bryce just stared at her blankly.

"Hey, what's up?" Dixyn said, breaking the ice.

"Nuttin'," he replied. "What's up with you?"

"Hangin' in there, I guess."

"You guess? I barely talk to you and you ain't come to see me since I've been locked up, and the first thing you got to tell me is you hangin' in there, *you guess?*"

Part of Dixyn wanted to come straight out and tell Bryce everything, from the stripping to dealing with his conniving brother. She wanted to tell him how fucked up of a predicament he had left her in. Yet she felt he probably had enough to deal with right now. Dixyn didn't want to burden him any further. So she let him vent. Today she would try to be the bigger person. "You miss me?" she asked lovingly.

"No," Bryce answered straight-faced. "How could I miss a chick who has minimum contact with me? She doesn't write, I can't call her. I've spoken to my attorney more than I have my so-called fiancée."

Despite what he was saying, Dixyn saw the truth in his eyes. They were filled with love, there was no denying it. "Bryce, you're full of shit, man. You just tryin' to break a bitch down, once again. If you only knew what I was goin' through just to keep a roof over my head—"

"Yo, where the hell is your ring?" he suddenly demanded.

A panicked expression flashed across Dixyn's face before she caught herself. "I got robbed," she said.

"What? Where? How come you ain't tell me?"

"Ummm . . . I was out with Kendra and her cousin. We went up to some club in DC to celebrate her birthday. When the club closed, some bama followed Kendra all the way back to the car, trying to holla at her. I guess he got mad 'cause he wasn't gettin' no play. Next thing I know I got a pistol pointed in my face. He talkin' 'bout *Take off the ring*."

"What?" Bryce shouted.

"Yep," Dixyn continued, "I wasn't the only one that he robbed. The bama robbed Kendra and her cousin too."

"For what?"

"A couple hundred dollars and they earrings," she said.

"Yo, you shouldn't been hangin' out wit' that cokehead bitch in the first place. If I were home, that wouldn't never have happened 'cause you wouldn't have been there. That bitch Kendra is bad news. Let this be a lesson to you to stay away from her."

Dixyn couldn't believe how masterfully she had crafted her story. She also couldn't believe how easily she had convinced Bryce. Any way you put it, she was glad that part was over. "Bryce, guess what?" Dixyn said. "Ya brother Brian is in town. He finally came."

She watched as Bryce's face twisted up into a sour expression. "Word?" he responded, shaking his head in disbelief. "That nigga's in town and he ain't come to see me? Yo, stay away from him."

Following Bryce's orders wouldn't be so easy for Dixyn. Her interactions with B-Dub were out of financial necessity, not choice. "But babe, that's ya brother, I thought you said he'd have my back. What's goin' on with y'all?"

"Listen, I can't git into all that over this jack. These walls have ears, know what I'm sayin'? Don't trust my brother. The nigga is no good. If he weren't my blood, I wouldn't even fuck wit' him."

Bryce paced back and forth in the holding cell like he was losing his mind as the memories flooded back: Hours after the police had raided his Harlem tenement building, arresting him, his younger brother Brian, and his mother Bernice, Bryce still couldn't believe it. Despite receiving several warnings from old hustlers about shitting where he ate, he'd continued making drug transactions out of his building. The money had been so good he couldn't bring himself to close down his operation. So what Bryce couldn't bring himself to do, the police did themselves, shutting him down and taking two innocent people to jail with him in the process. The police had gone through the Winters's apartment with a fine-tooth comb until they found two ounces of crack hidden in a stash can, a hollow-bottomed coffee container, in the kitchen.

"Hey, Tweedledum, here's your brother Tweedledee," a policeman announced as he opened the cell door. "You two geniuses figure out who's gonna take the rap for that crack we found at your apartment. It's a goddamn shame you's two assholes had to involve your mother in all this. Christ, if I had sons like you, I'd disown 'em. You got five minutes to talk it out. One of you's is going home and the other is going to jail."

Bryce recklessly eyeballed the police officer. All he could think about at the moment was how much he hated the cops. They always had some slick shit to say to him. Right now he wasn't feeling it.

The cop shrugged off Bryce's dirty look; he just smirked and walked off.

"So what we gon' do?" Brian asked.

"What you mean *we*, bro?" Bryce replied as a knot formed in his stomach. "Yo, this is my beef, not yours. You and Ma ain't have nuttin' to do wit' dis."

"Yo, Bryce, don't be stupid," Brian said. "My nigga, you still on five years' probation from that gun charge. If your probation officer gets wind of this, you goin' up north. You gon' do at least three to six . . ."

Until then, Bryce hadn't even bothered to consider the time he was facing. He forgot all about being on unsupervised probation. He'd been too stressed about getting his younger brother and mother arrested.

"Yo, I got this, fam," Brian told him. "Yo, officer, come back 'round here and cut my brother and mother loose."

Secretly, Brian had always wanted to be a hustler, but Bryce never let him. He didn't want to just do the nickel-and-dime, scratching and scrapping for re-up money either. He wanted to be a big-time hustler like Nicky Barnes or Rich Porter, a local celebrity, respected and admired by everyone, not just in his neighborhood, but all of Harlem.

Before Bryce could protest, the policeman was at the cell door. "I'm glad one of you's dirtbags came to your senses. Your poor mother is in the interrogation room crying her eyes out," the cop said, opening the door.

Inwardly, Bryce breathed a sigh of relief as he exited the cell. "I got you, bro," he proclaimed. "You ain't gon' want for nuttin'."

After Brian took the weight for his brother, the whole family came down on him. Some family members swore never to talk to Brian again. Even his own mother became distant. No amount of arguing and explaining could convince them of his innocence. Brian suddenly became the black sheep. This was the thanks he got for helping his big brother out of a jam.

Bryce was supposed to get him a paid attorney, but he never did. It took a little longer than expected for him to recover from the losses he suffered as a result of the raid. By the time he got back on his feet, B-Dub was up for sentencing. Without a good lawyer, he was sentenced to one to three years in a New York State correctional institution. Thus began an intense and lasting sibling rivalry.

From that point on, B-Dub's life essentially spiraled downward into a life of pure crime. And he felt his brother owed him big time.

* * *

"Just tell me why. Why you talkin' all crazy 'bout your brother?" she demanded.

"Cain killed Abel," Bryce replied. "Did he not? And weren't they brothers?"

Dixyn paused for a moment. She had not expected this. Now she was starting to see things from a different angle. Still, she didn't know what larger conclusions could be drawn from the conversation. But what she did know was that she was going to heed Bryce's advice. If B-Dub's own brother had such choice words for him, they had to be based on something.

Somehow they managed to change the topic to Ava. Dixyn told him how well she was speaking, how tall she'd grown, all the progress their daughter was making under her mother's tutelage. Bryce began talking about their relationship and all the things they needed to do to strengthen their bond, like staying in touch more often. The couple even reminisced about happier times. Although Dixyn knew that Bryce was facing a lengthy sentence, she tried to remain optimistic, hoping things could somehow work themselves out for the better. Yet deep down she knew this was unlikely.

Dixyn exited the jail with a funny feeling in pit of her stomach. She wasn't sure she and Bryce could stand the test of time, especially if he ever found out the truth about her and B-Dub. It was like they were now headed in opposite directions, living in separate realities.

Dixyn took the long way home to clear her mind and think at length about both Bryce and B-Dub. She could still hear Bryce's voice in her head: *Don't trust my brother. The nigga is no good.*

CHAPTER EIGHT

Kendra swung by Dixyn's house to pick her up for the bachelor party. Dixyn preferred that they ride to-gether rather than meeting her there. She wanted everything to go as smoothly as possible. Kendra had a reputation for being notoriously late, but tonight she was right on time. As she pulled into Dixyn's drive, she glanced at her watch to be sure. It read 9 p.m.

"Damn, where fuck is this bitch at?" she cursed aloud to herself, then reached into her cup holder and grabbed her cell phone. She pressed a button and the phone rang a few times before Dixyn answered.

"Where are you, Dix? We on a tight schedule here. You need to get to the front door ASAP."

"I'm comin' down now."

Dixyn eyed the row of stilettos shoes lined up neatly against the wall of her walk-in closet. She had acquired several pairs of "fuck-me heels," as Kendra referred to them, over the past few months. But tonight she couldn't make up her mind which shoes to pack. She contemplated whether to keep it simple with a pair of sexy black six-inch heels or to go with her personal favorite, the hot-pink ones with the highest arch. With Kendra waiting impatiently, she went with her initial instinct, grabbing the black pair and putting them in her bag.

"What's good, Ken?" Dixyn asked as she slipped inside the car.

"You!" Kendra snapped. "I told you to be ready when I got here. I get here and you're nowhere to be found."

"C'mon, you of all people should know women take a long time to get their shit together. My bad, it wasn't like I was purposely trying to be late."

"Don't worry about it," Kendra replied. "Never mind me. I just wanna make sure we get there on time to get all this money." Shaking off her annoyance, she backed out of the driveway and concentrated on the road. She wanted to get to Crystal City, Virginia, as quickly as possible. As Kendra merged onto the highway, she finally felt relaxed enough to strike up a conversation.

"Guess what?"

"What?"

Kendra began, "You not goin' to believe this. A couple hours afta you left the club the police raided that joint."

"You lyin'?"

"Girl, I wish. I was there when it happened. Like a hundred cops, sheriffs, and state troopers busted up in there. Muthafuckas started emptyin' they pockets, throwin' drugs and other illegal shit on the fuckin' floor, stashin' shit in the seats. It was crazy."

"Wwwwhhhhhaaaaaat? I'm glad I left when I did."

"That's not all. Guess what else happened?"

"What?" Dixyn replied.

"They arrested Notti," Kendra said. "They walked his ass upstairs to his office."

"What they arrest him for? What did he do?"

"I heard it was for some drugs they found up in his office. All I know is I saw them escort his fat ass upstairs, then a few minutes later they bought him back down in cuffs."

"Wow!" Dixyn gasped. Her mind flashed back to the heated conversation she'd overheard between Notti and B-Dub. His harsh words toward Notti hadn't been empty threats. He had made good on them after all. Rather than sharing what she knew with Kendra, however, Dixyn decided to keep it to herself, especially having seen firsthand what happened to people who crossed B-Dub.

"Listen, that ain't the half of it. They brought in drug-sniffin' dogs and searched the entire club, bathroom, locker room, and all. They ran everybody's name for warrants, and if you had one, they took ya ass in," Kendra explained.

Dixyn listened intently, letting her imagination paint the picture of the police raid. "Did a lot of people get locked up?"

"Not as many as you might think. Nobody you know. Anyway, what happened to you last night?" Kendra asked. "Wasn't you supposed to go see Notti in his office?"

"I was goin' up there, but on the way I spotted this guy I knew from back in the day, so I went outside and hid in my car for a while. By the time he finally left, I decided to leave too."

"Fa real? Notti told me to tell you that if you plan on continuin' to work at the club, then you need to show up more often, not whenever you feel like it. He said the next time you don't show up when you're scheduled to work, don't bother comin' back."

Dixyn wasn't too concerned. She had heard Notti issue similar threats to a few other girls. Strip joints in the DC area were a dime a dozen. If Notti fired her, she could take her show on the road if need be.

"I guess you don't have to worry about that now. His fat ass got bigger problems to deal with than worryin' 'bout you, like getting the hell outta the county jail."

"You got that right," Dixyn said.

"If you ask me, I think the nigga was bluffin'. He been sayin' the same shit to different bitches for years. You know what I say, right? Fuck 'em. I'm tired of talkin' 'bout his sorry ass."

Dixyn was happy to drop the subject. "So Kendra, lemme ask you something. Are we gonna be the only chicks there?"

"Of course not," Kendra responded. "Fonda and Chocolate is meetin' us there. You know Chocolate, right?"

"I know of her, like who she is, but I don't know her personally."

"Well, don't worry, she cool peeps. 'Bout her money like everybody else," Kendra assured her.

In Dixyn's mind the term "about her money" could only mean one thing: Chocolate was down for anything and everything. *Chocolate will fuck for a buck and do something strange for some change.* She was officially one of *them*, which meant Dixyn would need to figure out a way to make some extra money without compromising her morals to get it.

Dixyn watched from the car as Kendra walked into the office of the Red Roof Inn. After saying a few words to the motel manager, she handed over her identification and credit card. Roughly five minutes later, Kendra exited the office with a room key in hand. Dixyn noticed that she was texting someone while she walked toward the car.

"What are we doin' here?" Dixyn asked. "I thought we were doin' the bachelor party."

"We are. We're doin' it right here," Kendra said. "To be on the safe side, I thought it was best if we didn't travel to these dudes' hood. Then we might get all type of undesirables crashin' the party. I don't got time to be dealin' with no broke niggas. They take a bitch through too many changes. They want a whole lot for a li'l bit."

For a split second, Dixyn considered going right back home; things weren't unfolding like she thought they would be. Yet she quickly dispelled the notion when she remembered she wasn't the one driving. And suddenly she also saw the logic in Kendra's plan. She felt safe, if only for the moment, so she didn't question her friend any further.

Kendra and Dixyn grabbed their respective duffle bags from the trunk and entered the motel room. It was clean and spacious, though nothing to brag about. For what they had in mind, it would definitely do. Immediately, Kendra dialed up her clients and gave them the address to the motel. Then the two women settled into the room and began unpacking their outfits for the night. They took turns freshening up in the bathroom before the guests arrived.

Kendra whipped out a bottle of Cîroc Coconut vodka along with a small bottle of cranberry juice and a can of Red Bull. They each got a nice little buzz off the liquor before moving to harder drugs. Dixyn rolled up a blunt while Kendra indulged herself in powder cocaine. Between Dixyn's tokes and Kendra's snorting, the girls enjoyed light conversation.

"Dix, I'm tellin' you, these niggas got money. Every time they come to the club they make it rain."

"Ken, where's Fonda and Chocolate at? We been here for a while and they still ain't show up."

Kendra shrugged. "Ya guess is as good as mine. Lemme call these bitches. They shoulda been here by now." She grabbed her cell phone and with the touch of a button was connected to her road dog. "Bitch, where are you?"

"Hold ya muthafuckin' horses. I'm pullin' up right now," Fonda answered.

Moments later there was a knock on the door to the

adjoining room. Kendra strolled over and opened the door. Fonda and Chocolate entered.

Almost immediately the two women started getting high. Dixyn chuckled to herself; being sober clearly wasn't one of their priorities at the moment.

"Sure took y'all bitches long enough to git here," Kendra chirped.

"Talk to Ms. I'm-Comin'-Right-Down here," Fonda said, nodding her head in Chocolate's direction.

"Looks like we both had the same problem. Ol' Dixyn here took her own sweet time too," Kendra said.

"Kendra!" Dixyn was annoyed.

"Bitch, am I lyin'? Anyway, let's start gettin' ready. These niggas will be here soon."

Quickly all four women donned the skimpy outfits they would be wearing to start off the evening, then re-applied makeup and touched up their hair again.

It was almost twelve o'clock when the guests began to arrive. Well-dressed men, wearing the latest in urban fashions, pulled up in high-end luxury cars with Washington, DC license plates. They all arrived within a few minutes of each other. These guys were definitely ballers.

Kendra sure knows how to pick 'em, Dixyn thought. She watched closely from the bathroom, making sure she didn't know any of the dudes and, more importantly, none of them knew her.

"Okay, guys, it's party time," Kendra announced to the half dozen men in attendance. "Don't be shy, get ya freak on. We here to turn ya fantasies into realities."

From a portable radio in the corner, "Rack City" by

rapper Tyga began to flow from the speakers, enhancing the mood: sins of the flesh and lots of it. The girls shook their asses, twerking all over the room. The atmosphere was tame at first, but after the weed and liquor came into play, it got pretty wild.

Fonda and Chocolate performed oral sex on one guy at the same time. This got almost every man's attention. They showered them with money, and some whipped out their phones and snapped pictures. While all this was going on, Kendra disappeared into the adjoining room for what Dixyn assumed was a quick fuck or VIP act. Dixyn settled in for a lap dance with a client in the corner. She was gearing up to take drastic measures like her cohorts. She let him dry hump on her ass till he busted a nut in his pants.

Hours after getting everything they wanted, the men still lingered around, smoking, drinking, watching sex shows performed by Kendra, Fonda, or Chocolate. They were engaging in oral sex, even doing each other at the same damn time. These women performed every sexual act conceivable.

Of course, this was exactly what Kendra wanted. The longer the men stayed, the more money they spent.

But suddenly, without any warning, three masked men burst into the room from the darkness of the adjoining room carrying semiautomatic handguns with silencers attached. Panic swept the room.

Dixyn froze and put her hands high in the air but stayed right where she was, on some dude's lap.

"Niggas, y'all hit the muthafuckin' floor! Bitches, y'all get on the muthafuckin' bed," one of the gunmen barked, tightening his grip on his weapon.

The intruders hovered over the men like birds of prey, waiting for anyone to make a false move while scanning the room for valuables.

"Give it up!" another gunman yelled. "We want watches, chains, bracelets, earrings, money, every muthafuckin' thing, fam."

Dixyn's ears perked up. There was only one dude she knew who threw that last word around. She made it a point to discretely keep an eye on him.

At gunpoint, the men were robbed of any valuables they had on them. Then they were ordered to strip off every item of clothing and lay on the floor to prevent them from giving chase once the bandits made their escape. Most of the men complied, but one of them refused.

"I ain't takin' my muthafuckin' clothes off, Joe," he said. "Fa what? Y'all already got e'rything we had on us, from our money to our cars keys. Naw . . ."

A lone gunman walked over to him and shoved his pistol into the back of the guy's head. "You got five seconds to take off your clothes or I'm gonna blow ya muthafuckin' head off!" he snarled. "One, two, three, four . . ."

Before the gunman could finish his count, the guy made his move. He tried to roll over onto his back and snatch the gun. Unfortunately, he wasn't quick enough to disarm his captor. From point-blank range, the gunman fired two shots into his head, killing him instantly. Mayhem ensued as the other attackers started randomly firing on the other partygoers.

Dixyn's pulse began to pound. She stared in horror at the scene before her, images of blood and brain matter burning into her subconscious. She clamped her hand over her own mouth, stifling the sounds involuntarily coming out.

"Shut the fuck up, bitch! Or you next," a gunman warned, pointing his pistol in their direction.

Huddled closely together, each woman silently said a prayer that this wasn't the night that they would meet their maker.

"Dixyn, Dixyn, are you okay?" Kendra asked while speeding down the highway. "Dixyn . . ."

She must have blacked out. She couldn't recollect how she'd gotten dressed, and more importantly, how she'd escaped the motel with her life. When she came to, she was in the passenger seat of Kendra's car, glancing nervously into the side mirror. Dixyn didn't really know what to say. This situation was different from anything she'd ever dealt with before. This wasn't just any old ordinary crime. This was murder, and somehow she was involved in it.

"I'm good," she finally replied, still in a daze. "Kendra . . . Kendra, what the hell just happened back there?"

"Honestly, Dixyn, I don't know," Kendra said. "It wasn't supposed to happen like that . . ."

"What do you mean?" Dixyn shot back. "Wasn't *supposed to* happen?"

Kendra clammed up. "Nuttin'," she said.

"Kendra, one of them dudes' voices sounded real familiar. One of them was B-Dub, right? I didn't know you knew him."

Suddenly Dixyn realized the connection between the two. She thought about all the recent run-ins she'd had with the two of them—influencing her to strip, B-Dub's sudden appearance at the club, the transportation of his guns, and now the incident tonight. Everything didn't seem so coincidental anymore.

Kendra ignored Dixyn, choosing to remain silent. For now she would let her assume whatever she wanted to assume.

Dixyn stared at her in disbelief. She could see the uneasiness in her friend's face. "Kendra, you don't gotta say another muthafuckin' word. I ain't as stupid as you think I am!" Dixyn spat. "I know . . . and it's fucked up that you would even involve me in some shit like this. What about my daughter?"

Once again, Kendra didn't respond.

As far as Dixyn was concerned, she had her entire life ahead of her, and that of her daughter. She couldn't afford to have her future snatched away because she was an accessory to a murder. Making money was one thing, but committing serious crimes was something totally different. She was done—done with Kendra, done with B-Dub, done with the entire strip club scene. This wasn't for her anymore. Dixyn was not about this life.

For several minutes, neither Kendra nor Dixyn uttered a word to each other. Kendra concentrated on driving. The farther away she got from the scene of the crime, the more relaxed she became. Meanwhile, the more Dixyn thought about the incident, the angrier she grew.

"I'm sicka this shit!" Dixyn eventually snapped. "I want out."

"Why you wanna do that for? This is easy money. And you know you need the money."

"Kendra, unlike you, I can't put a dollar amount on my life," Dixyn stated.

"I think you blowin' things way outta proportion," Kendra quickly responded.

"*Outta proportion* . . ." Dixyn repeated, her voice trailing off. "A nigga gets killed right in front of my face and I'm blowin' things outta proportion? No, you, B-Dub, and whoever those other niggas wit' guns were outta control!"

"Remember how fucked up you were before B-Dub came along?" Kendra said. "He just tryin' to help you . . ."

Dixyn couldn't believe her ears. Suddenly she knew she had confided in the wrong person. She could only shake her head. This disagreement was more than merely a difference of opinion. Dixyn now figured that because of Kendra's ever-present drug use, her allegiance could easily be bought. And she remembered a time when Kendra had been closer than a regular friend, more like a sister, when she could tell her everything. It seemed that time had come and gone.

* * *

Kendra carefully parked her car between two others at the Waffle House somewhere in Virginia. The place was packed with late-night partygoers and people who had just left the local bar and wanted to grab a bite before calling it a night.

"What are we doin' here?" Dixyn asked. "How could you think about eatin' at a time like this?"

"Get out the car. We not here to eat. We here to meet B-Dub," Kendra told her.

Dixyn didn't move a muscle. She looked at Kendra like she had lost her mind. Meeting B-Dub was the last thing she wanted to do. She wanted to stay as far away from that guy as possible. There was no way she was going to a meeting with that lowlife.

"Bitch, you better come on if you want your money," Kendra warned.

Dixyn reconsidered her stance. She wanted and needed her money. Without it, the night was a total waste. Reluctantly, she climbed out of the car and joined Kendra as they walked the short distance to the entrance.

After a quick scan of the crowded restaurant, they spotted B-Dub sitting alone in a booth. He waved for them to come over and join him.

"Dixyn," B-Dub cheerfully greeted, "what's good? Long time no see."

Dixyn stared at him coldly as she took a seat across from him. Kendra took the seat right next to him.

"Why so mean?" he asked. "Okay, maybe this will put a smile on ya face, fam." B-Dub removed a wad of

money from his hoodie pocket and handed it over to Dixyn.

She accepted the money and put it away, careful not to draw attention to herself. She knew it was more than what she'd been expecting. It was hush money.

"I don't appreciate that shit y'all pulled back there," Dixyn whispered, still looking him directly in the eye.

B-Dub remained unfazed. He was calm and collected. He merely smirked back at her.

"Y'all didn't have to do that. One of us could have gotten seriously hurt."

"My bad, fam," he finally said. "Shit got outta hand. My guy went a li'l overboard."

"You think?" Dixyn replied sarcastically. She couldn't believe that someone had lost their life and all he had to say in his own defense was "my bad." Bryce had certainly been right about him. B-Dub was a cold, calculating, useless piece of shit who Dixyn now deemed unfit to walk the face of this earth.

"Next time it won't be like this. You'll see," B-Dub said.

Dixyn was astonished. First, she couldn't believe that he'd so quickly owned up to his part in the robbery/homicide. Second, he was crazy if he thought she would ever willingly involve herself in something like this again. "Sorry to burst ya bubble, but there won't be a next time for me," Dixyn countered. "Whatever you, Kendra, and whoever else got goin' on, I don't want any part of it."

Dixyn glanced at Kendra, who seemed unnerved by the conversation, not meeting her gaze. This was an

A-and-B conversation and Kendra seemed more than content to stay out of it.

"Listen, bitch," B-Dub snarled in a low tone, "you gonna do what the fuck I tell you to do, when I tell you to do it. Comprende? Unless you want me to go out to that fuckin' jail and give my dear ol' brother a blow-by-blow account of what you've been doin' out here in these streets since he's been gone. And take it from me, he ain't gonna be feelin' you one bit when I put my spin on this shit. He'll probably even disown the baby too. I'll have his ass askin' you for a paternity test."

Dixyn managed to muster some defiance: "Go to hell, muthafucka! I ain't tryin' to hear shit from you. B-Dub, you're the last person that needs to be tellin' me anything!"

"Look, Dixyn, shit is real, if you haven't noticed. If you're not wit' us, you're against us. And you saw tonight what happens to those who go against us."

"Are you threatening me?" she asked, raising her voice.

"Nah, Dixyn, I'm not threatenin' you, fam. I ain't gonna lay a fuckin' finger on you. There's a lotta different ways of hurtin' a person without gettin' physical. Know what I'm sayin'?"

Dixyn didn't know exactly what B-Dub meant by this, but she didn't like how it sounded. She felt as if she were being forced into some kind of indentured servitude. Should she admit to Bryce exactly what was going on, or turn to the police for help? Neither option sounded too appealing. For better or worse, Dixyn had a serious decision to make.

She suddenly felt alone in a world filled with enemies. She glared across the table at her tormenters, studying their faces, trying to glimpse some sense of humanity hidden deep within their souls, but she saw nothing. As for Kendra, or what remained of her, she was an empty shell of the former friend she once knew.

Feeling suffocated by the immense pressure she was under, Dixyn silently rose from the table, exited the restaurant, and walked out into the cool night air to clear her head. Through the glass, she could see Kendra and B-Dub engrossed in conversation. For the first time, she was truly ashamed of the life she was living. Her conscience began to eat at her. She thought about all the illicit activities she had involved herself in and the damage it had done to her, not physical but spiritual. This wasn't how she was raised; Dixyn wasn't about that life. She felt trapped. She began desperately searching the crevices of her brain for a way out of this mess.

CHAPTER NINE

T he body lay in a pool of blood. Dixyn jumped off the bed and immersed herself in warm bodily fluid in a valiant attempt to save the man's life. The extremity of the situation suggested that she panic or flee like everyone else had, yet she didn't. Blood stained her body and her hands. Dixyn saw her bloody palm print on the man's shirt as she felt his heart for any signs of life. Nothing. One look at his discolored face and hollow eyes and Dixyn knew he was already dead.

Suddenly she came to her senses and rose unsteadily to her feet, fighting hard to keep her footing in the vast amount of blood. Nearly falling several times, Dixyn finally made her way to the door. As she left the motel room, she came face to face with her worst fear: the cops. To her immediate left and right, she could see they had taken up tactical positions, crouching low with their weapons trained on her.

"Police! Freeze!" one cop barked. "Put your hands in the air where we can see them!"

It was a surreal moment. Dixyn was dazed by the swirl of

red and blue lights and everything else happening around her. She couldn't process their order to surrender. As it began to register, she wandered aimlessly toward the cops, her entire body drenched in blood.

"It wasn't me! I didn't do it!" she yelled.

"Miss, I'm warning you, don't take another step forward. Put your hands where I can see them."

"I didn't do nuttin'!" she cried, steadily advancing.

As the drama escalated, several more cop cars arrived on the scene, bringing with them reinforcements. Dixyn could feel her heartbeat quickening and let out a bloodcurdling scream. Yet still she kept advancing.

Fearing the woman was mentally deranged, the cops braced themselves for the worst. Their fingers tightened around their triggers as adrenaline pulsated through their bodies.

Even with several guns pointed at her, Dixyn didn't feel threatened. Then the loud crackle of gunfire stopped her dead in her tracks. One bullet after another pierced her body, and her blood flowed profusely as she dropped to the ground. Cops closed in on her body from all sides. As they hovered over her with their weapons trained, Dixyn could feel her soul slowly leaving her body.

Dixyn jerked awake, wide-eyed, sweating profusely, holding her heart. She shook her head and slowly fell back onto the softness of her bed. She was physically refreshed yet mentally wasted. Her thoughts were still wrapped up in the disturbing images of the murder at the bachelor party. Try as she might to detach herself from the event, she just couldn't.

What she did next was no different from any ordinary day. Dixyn took a shower, put on her clothes, went downstairs, and made herself some breakfast. After picking through her food, she pushed her plate away and sat back in the chair. Her mind wandered for a few moments before she decided to go into the living room to watch some television. She channel-surfed until something caught her eye.

"One man is dead as the Crystal City police begin to search for clues. Right behind me is the Red Roof Inn, where police say sometime last night twenty-six-year-old Eric Johnson of Washington, DC was found slain. The circumstances that led to his death were not immediately evident. Some occupants of the motel say they heard loud music coming from the room in question. There seemed to be some sort of party or celebration taking place in room 129 last night. However, there was no report of gunshots or even a scuffle. Police are combing the room for clues and interviewing guests who may have heard or seen something that could possibly guide them in this murder investigation. For now, there are no suspects, but police say they do have a license plate number from a car of a person of interest. But they're not making it public right now. Reporting live from Crystal City, this is Warren Scott, Fox 5 Morning News."*

Dixyn panicked and began feeling sick to her stomach. The image of the dead man once again flashed before her eyes. She picked up her phone and dialed Kendra's number. The phone rang for what seemed like an eternity with no response.

Unable to sit still in her home for another second, Dixyn got up off the couch and grabbed her purse and cars keys. She headed for the local 7-Eleven to buy a newspaper. She scanned the front page until she found what she was looking for, then drove home, anxious to check out the full article. Back at her place, she read the story several times, letting the reporter's words fill her brain.

Police say it was a bachelor party gone wrong. By the end of the night, one man lay shot, bleeding to death on the hotel floor. Just what provoked such a random act of violence, law enforcement officials can only speculate. Anyone with any information that may lead to the arrest of these suspects has been asked to call . . .

For the next few hours, Dixyn sat alone in her living room, lost in thought. She didn't know what to make of what had happened last night or where all the newfound trouble could possibly lead. Instinctively, Dixyn bowed her head and prayed for the soul that had been lost. She prayed that God would forgive her for the sins she had committed that led to this murder.

Dixyn dozed off with the newspaper neatly folded in her lap. When the ringing of her cell phone pulled her out of sleep, she saw that night had fallen. She had lost all track of time. Dixyn clumsily reached for her phone on a nearby night table and checked the screen. It was Kendra. Now Dixyn was wide awake.

"Kendra?"

"It's on!" the woman squealed.

"What? What are you talkin' about?"

"The club! It's already back open. Under new management, from what I heard. Notti's wife supposedly took over."

Dixyn shook her head in disbelief. Kendra truly had a one-track mind. "Look, we need to talk," Dixyn said. "I don't know if you are aware, but a lot of things have happened since last night, and it ain't all good."

Kendra went silent for a moment on the other end of the phone. "Hold ya horses," she finally replied. "Let's not talk about that over the phone. You never know who's listening. Come down to the club tonight and we'll talk. Face to face."

The telephone line went dead. Dixyn needed to talk to her, so she resigned herself to meeting up later that night in the noisy confines of the strip club.

When Dixyn got to the club that night, she found Chocolate and Fonda working the crowd. They saw her but barely acknowledged her. Dixyn could care less. She didn't like either one of them anyway. But the problem was, they were all in this together. She grinned at them and kept moving.

Dixyn spotted Kendra creeping down the stairs that led to Notti's office, although it appeared that the woman was trying her best to avoid her. Dixyn walked over and confronted her. "Kendra, let's find somewhere private to talk."

"Holla at me later. I got some business I gotta take care of," Kendra replied.

"I need to speak to you now," Dixyn insisted. "It's important." She grabbed Kendra's arm and pulled her back to the locker room. Once there, Dixyn reached inside her purse and handed Kendra a folded copy of the newspaper. "That shit made the news *and* the paper," she whispered.

Kendra simply shrugged her shoulders and passed the newspaper back to Dixyn.

"Well, what we gonna do?"

"Nuttin'!" Kendra snapped. "The police ain't got nuttin'. If they did, they woulda came and got us already. I'm not hidin' and neither are you, so that right there should tell you somethin'. All they have is a dead body, and last I checked, dead men don't talk."

Dixyn stared at Kendra blankly as she tried to make sense of what she had just heard. "It's only a matter of time. Investigations take time. Ain't you seen *CSI* before?" she said. "It might not happen today or tomorrow, but you *will* get arrested."

"Good," Kendra coolly replied. "Then let them muthafuckas do they job. When they do, they gon' know that I ain't shoot nobody. And if they don't, I'll tell 'em."

How Dixyn wished that things were that simple. Part of her wanted to just run away and hide till things blew over. But she couldn't bear the thought of leaving her daughter behind. She knew she had to stay, come what may.

"I don't know," Dixyn muttered. "I don't know if this is the right way to handle this situation."

"Since you obviously got this all figured out," Kendra responded with sarcasm, "what do you suppose we do?"

"I . . . I . . . I don't know," Dixyn stuttered. "I was hopin' we could put our heads together and come up with somethin'."

SHANNON HOLMES

Kendra merely sighed before marching off.

At that moment, Dixyn made up her mind that this was the last time she would ever attempt to talk sense into Kendra. From here on out, it was every woman for herself.

Dixyn took to the stage and stared out into the sea of hungry men anxiously waiting for her to gyrate her body to the rhythm of the beat and expose herself for all to see. As she slid up and down the pole, she stopped watching the crowd and focused solely on her own thoughts. *This is what my life has come to: sleep, eat, and strip.* Unlike a lot of the other girls, she neither loved nor lived for the job. Right now it simply paid the bills. This wasn't who she was; it was just something she happened to be doing. *This is my last night,* Dixyn promised herself. The sooner this was done, the better off she would be.

But as the night wore on, Dixyn found it hard to concentrate on dancing. She was burdened by what she had done and what she felt compelled to do now. No amount of money she made tonight could take her mind off of the murder investigation.

While Dixyn went through the motions onstage, Kendra was upstairs in the office with B-Dub.

"B, we gotta problem," Kendra announced. The urgency and nervousness she hadn't shown to her friend was on full display now. "That shit hit the papers. Dixyn told me she saw it on the news . . ."

B-Dub remained silent as Kendra filled him in on the

details. He was pondering ways to get himself out of this jam. And he came to one conclusion: kill the girls. They were the weak links. If the police got hold of them, he wasn't sure which one would snitch first. Since no one else knew his partners in crime, the brunt of the blame would fall squarely on him.

"Kendra, calm down. Everything is going to be all right," B-Dub soothed. "Now go back downstairs, fam, and keep an eye on our friend Dixyn. I got some business to handle up here. I'll holla back at you by the end of the night."

"Okay," Kendra responded obediently, then turned to exit the office.

"Here," B-Dub called out to her. "Take a few of these to calm ya'self down."

Kendra extended her hand and B-Dub dumped about a half dozen pills in her palm. Kendra balled up her hand into a tight fist and rushed out of the office.

As B-Dub looked on, he couldn't help but think, *Junkie bitch!* He knew exactly how to get rid of her when the time came. Dealing with the other girls required some thought.

By the time Dixyn had gotten dressed to head home, Kendra, Fonda, and Chocolate were nowhere to be found. This didn't bother Dixyn one bit; she hoped to never see them again. She was happy to leave those bitches right where she found them. It was over between her and stripping. It was a relationship that had been doomed from the start. Without regret, Dixyn left every stripper outfit and every other item associated with stripping that she had bought inside her locker. *Good riddance,* she thought as she departed the locker room for the final time.

Fonda and Chocolate pulled up to the local Sheetz convenience store to get a few refreshments and blunt wraps for their weed. Fonda stayed in the car texting, trying to salvage a date she had lined up for later that evening. Meanwhile, Chocolate headed inside the store. Each woman was too engrossed in her own task to notice the tinted late-model black Honda Accord that pulled slowly into the packed lot.

Unable to spot her roommate through the store glass, Fonda called her phone. "Bitch, where are you? What's taking you so long?"

"Bitch, I'm in da bathroom," Chocolate fired back. "I had to pee. Is that all right wit' you?"

"Hurry da fuck up!" Fonda said, sucking her teeth.

Within a few minutes, Chocolate returned to the car with a large grocery bag.

"Now I see what really took you so long. You practically bought the whole gotdamn store."

"Your period must be about to come down, 'cause all you been doin' is complaining ever since we left the club," Chocolate replied. "Lemme roll up dis blunt. Maybe that'll keep ya ass from trippin'."

Chocolate sat in the passenger's seat and prepared the blunt while Fonda kept a sharp eye out for the police. Chocolate soon sparked up the blunt and they pulled out of the parking lot.

Since they were smoking, they didn't want to run the risk of getting pulled over. Fonda made a detour off the main thoroughfare and took the back roads home.

They passed the blunt between them. Billows of smoke poured out of the car as each woman took hearty pulls. The weed was beginning to make Fonda horny. Although she didn't have any dick lined up for the night, Chocolate would more than suffice. They had hooked up on more than a few occasions, inside and outside the club, and it had always been memorable. True to form, Fonda reached over and caressed Chocolate's breasts, letting her know what time it was.

"Okay," Chocolate mumbled between tokes. "Now you talkin'." To Chocolate, it was all in good fun, and she had given as well as she had gotten.

Aroused, Fonda began to accelerate to get home more quickly. Suddenly a pair of headlights appeared in the rearview mirror. They were so high that they hadn't even noticed the car following them until it was too late. Fonda slowed her vehicle down. As soon as the other car pulled within a few feet of them, Fonda quickly determined that this was not a police car after all. The vehicle flashed its high beams and then sped up as if to pass them. As both cars pulled even with each other, the car in question suddenly veered right and slammed into them.

"What the fuck?" Fonda rasped.

When it happened again, Fonda immediately knew this was a life-or-death situation and floored it. The two cars raced up the narrow road.

Fonda and Chocolate were nervous wrecks inside their vehicle as they struggled to make sense of what was happening. Fonda tried not to let her friend's screams distract her. Her mind was racing, yet she managed to focus completely on the road, thinking about everything and nothing at all.

"Drive, Fonda, drive!" Chocolate shrieked.

Fonda's eyes began to tear up. She had to blink numerous times to clear her vision. The revving of car engines was all that could be heard on the otherwise empty back road. The chase car tapped Fonda's from the back, attempting to fishtail it. Fonda reacted badly, mashing her foot on the gas.

The darkness of night was doing a perfect job of camouflaging the sharp turn in the road up ahead.

Fonda was still driving at high speed when she hit the curve. She cut the steering wheel hard—too hard. She lost control of the car and it violently tumbled, rolling numerous times before it came to rest upside down in a ditch. The sick, twisted wreckage suddenly burst into a ball of flames, thus sealing the occupants' doom.

Slowly the chase car rolled past the scene of the accident. If the crash didn't kill the girls, surely the fire would. They calmly pulled away, secure in the knowledge that they had done their job.

And yet this was far from over. On the contrary, this was only the beginning.

CHAPTER TEN

It was going to be a good day. Dixyn told this to herself over and over from the time she opened her eyes. There was no indication that it wouldn't be. Her morning shower invigorated her. She treated herself to her favorite breakfast: cheese eggs, grits, and bacon. Her breakfast had never tasted so good. It was time to forget the murder, the strip club, and her fake friends. The sun was shining bright. It was the dawn of a new day, and she had to get on with her life.

Dixyn could have stayed at home all day and still found plenty more reasons to smile. But duty called in the form of motherhood, so it was off to her mother's to spend some quality time with Ava. Dixyn called ahead so her mother would be expecting her.

"Hello, Ma?" Dixyn said into the phone. "What are y'all doin'?"

"Nothing, Dixyn. Ava just running around the house driving me crazy. The usual. What are you up to?"

"Oh, I was on my way down there and I wanted to see if you guys were gonna be home before I came," she replied.

"Dixyn, you know you got my house keys, so even if we weren't here you could have let yourself in and waited for us."

"I know, Ma, I just didn't wanna surprise you no more like I did before. From here on out, I'm gonna start coming down there regularly until I'm able to bring my daughter back home."

"C'mon then. I'll tell Ava you're on your way," her mother said.

"Yes, do that. I'll see y'all soon."

Dixyn couldn't get to her mother's house fast enough. She was going to chill out in the country for a few days for some much-needed rest and relaxation.

Dixyn finally pulled into her mother's driveway. As soon as she inserted her key into the door, she heard the pitter-patter of small feet.

"Moooooommmmmmmyyyyy!" Ava yelled as she raced toward her mother.

Dixyn knelt down and extended her arms and Ava leaped into her embrace. It was tender moments like this that Dixyn truly missed the most. She wished she could walk back outside and reenter the house again and again. There was nothing in the world that she would trade this feeling for.

"Hey, Ava, I missed you so much, baby. You missed me?"

"I miss you too, Mommy. When you goin' ta take

me home? I wanna go back home with my mommy and daddy. Where Daddy? I don't see him in a long time."

"Daddy . . ." Dixyn began. "Daddy's away . . . Daddy's away at college."

"I thought my daddy finished school," Ava replied.

"No, he went back to study a few more things." Dixyn regretted needing to lie to her child. But it was her way of keeping *home* alive, her way of hoping Bryce didn't receive a lengthy sentence. She quickly changed the subject. "What you did you do today?"

"I watched TV and played a game on the 'puter. Come, Mommy, I'll show you the game." Ava took her mother's hand and led her straight to the living room.

Dixyn found her mother planted there on the sofa, her gaze fixed on the flat-screen television that hung on the wall. When Dixyn noticed how quiet and motionless her mother was, she knew this could only mean one thing: she was watching her daily dose of soap operas.

"Hey, Mom!" Dixyn called out, knowing that the greeting would annoy her mother. "Mom?"

"Shhhhh!" Mrs. Greene replied without even bothering to look at her daughter. She was totally engrossed in her favorite soap opera, *The Young and the Restless*, as she was every weekday around this time. "I'm trying to find out how Jack Abbott is gonna get out of this mess."

"Ma, you really need to quit watchin' these stories," Dixyn said. "Anyway, I thought I told you the best ones come on Friday and Monday. You could miss the rest of the week, just tune in on those two days and you'll find out everything you need to know."

"I been watchin' these stories since before you were alive and I'ma keep on watchin' them till the day I die," Mrs. Greene answered. "Now shhhhh! Leave me be, Dixyn."

Dixyn laughed off her mother's words. She knew there was nothing she could say or do that would dissuade her mother from watching her soap operas.

Dixyn sat down at the computer desk with Ava in her lap. She watched as her daughter maneuvered perfectly on the computer until she found the website she visited frequently to play games. Dixyn realized that when it was all said and done, Ava would be more computer savvy than she would ever be.

After a few minutes of watching her daughter play, Dixyn heard the theme music for the soap opera, signaling that the show was over. She eased up off the executive chair and walked over and took a seat next to her mom.

"Hello, Mother," Dixyn said cheerfully. "Is it safe to talk to you now? I'm not disturbing you or anything, am I?"

"Oh, chile, please. You of all people should know how I am about my stories."

"I know, Ma. I'm just playin' around wit' you."

Mrs. Greene smiled lovingly at her daughter. "What's going on, baby? You look different, better than the last time I saw you, like something's been lifted off your shoulders. How's everything?"

It was almost as if her mother could read her mind. *Mom knows best*, Dixyn thought. She didn't know where to start or if she even wanted to start at all.

"I've been under a lot of pressure since Bryce got arrested. I guess I took too much upon myself tryin' to be Superwoman and save the day. All the responsibilities, financially, that Bryce would normally take care of suddenly fell on me. Ma, you don't even know the half of it . . ." Dixyn let out a hard sigh. "Finally things seem to be working themselves out."

"Dixyn, you know God never gives you more than you can bear?" Mrs. Greene said. "Matthew 11:28–30: *Come to Me all you who are struggling hard and carrying heavy loads, and I will give you rest. Put on My yoke and learn from Me. I'm gentle and humble. And you will find rest for yourselves. My yoke is easy to bear, and My burden is light.*"

Dixyn wasn't the least bit surprised by her mom's statement. Her mom never missed a chance to impart some scripture on her. Any other time this might have annoyed her, but right now even Dixyn was beginning to think she needed the Lord in her life. "Mom, I fell in with the wrong crowd. I seen some things I shouldn't have seen. I been in some places that maybe I shouldn't have been. And all for what? Because I needed some money?"

"Dixyn, let your conscience be your guide. If it don't feel right, then it ain't right."

Dixyn felt like she lacked the moral compass her mother had given her to guide her life. Although stripping hadn't felt right, the financial results had been good. Their lives were totally different. Her mother had grown up in another time. The world had been a much simpler place back then. Right now she needed her mother more than ever. She didn't want a sermon; she didn't need to be judged. All Dixyn wanted was to be that little girl in her mother's arms all over again.

"I know I'm talkin' in riddles and you can't totally understand what I'm sayin'," Dixyn said. "Ma, I wish I could tell you everything. One day I will."

Mrs. Greene moved closer and gently held her daughter's hand, massaging it soothingly. She decided not to press Dixyn about the details. She had no idea what was going on. Dixyn would tell her everything as soon as she was good and ready, that she knew. For now, Mrs. Greene hoped that her presence and her touch were enough comfort to ease her daughter's mind.

Dixyn felt like a little girl all over again, a child trying to confess her way into forgiveness after doing a bad thing.

"You can talk to me, Dixyn, always remember that. Last time you were here I had a feeling that something was wrong. I'm here for you, just like I've always been, no matter what happened or who did what. I'm your mother and I love you unconditionally, just like you love that little girl over there."

Dixyn couldn't help the emotions from seeping through and began to cry.

"Everything is going to be all right," Mrs. Greene whispered into her daughter's ear as she hugged her.

After a few minutes of silent sobs, Dixyn regained her composure and she wiped away her tears. Ava was only a few feet away from them but didn't seem to have heard or witnessed the drama.

"You know me and Herman was going to our time-

share this weekend in Virginia Beach," Mrs. Greene announced. "We were going to bring Ava along, but now I
figure that you can take her back home with you for the
weekend. It seems like you could use the company."

Her mother was right. Dixyn certainly could use the
company. More importantly, she saw this as an opportunity to get reacclimated with her daughter and vice
versa. Yes, she would take Ava home and they would
spend some quality time together. In Dixyn's mind, this
would be the first in a series of steps toward bringing her
daughter home for good.

Mrs. Greene continued, "You're welcome to stay a
couple days until we leave. That way you can kill two
birds with one stone and spend time with both Ava *and*
me."

"Sounds like a plan," Dixyn agreed.

Dixyn had never particularly cared for the country.
She was a city girl at heart, albeit a small city. Her home-
town of Fredericksburg, Virginia was a city all the same.

Night after night she stayed up into the wee hours talking
to her daughter until Ava fell asleep. Then Dixyn would
just gaze out her window into the pitch blackness of the
woods. She didn't feel threatened by the nothingness she
saw. On the contrary, she felt relief. Dixyn had seen so
much over the course of a few weeks that seeing nothing
didn't bother her one bit.

As boring as it was out there, the fresh air and cool
breeze suited Dixyn just fine.

CHAPTER ELEVEN

As she got within a few exits of her home, Dixyn switched her phone back on. She was no longer concerned about the people she was trying to avoid. She realized that Bryce could have been trying to reach her for the last few days. If she missed his call, he'd probably go crazy, overcome by thoughts of infidelity. Dixyn didn't want him to think that about her. He had enough to deal with already.

Once her phone powered up, it seemed to erupt in a bevy of activity. She was besieged by missed calls and text messages, most of which were from her so-called friend Kendra. Dixyn didn't know what Kendra wanted with her, nor did she really care. She didn't have the time or energy to stay mentally vested in Kendra, B-Dub, or whatever was going on back at the club. She made a mental note to change her number that very day, as soon as she got settled in at home.

Almost on cue, the phone suddenly began to ring.

Absentmindedly, Dixyn answered without even checking to see who the caller was. "Hello? Who this?" she said slowly into the phone.

"Where the fuck you been? You sure took ya time about hittin' me back! What the fuck is good?" Kendra spat rapidly.

"I was away," Dixyn told her. "Let's just put it like that."

"Bitch, we need to talk! I got something to tell you."

"What? What do you have to tell me?

"Can't talk about it on the phone!" Kendra snapped.

"Why? What's the big deal?"

"It's somethin' we need to discuss face to face," Kendra insisted.

Dixyn could sense something was seriously wrong just by the tone of Kendra's voice. She sounded just like she had a few days earlier. On the strength of the past friendship, Dixyn agreed to get together with her and hear her out. "Meet me at my house," Dixyn said. "I'll be there in like fifteen minutes."

As Dixyn pulled up into her driveway, she saw two cars blocking her garage. One she easily recognized as Kendra's BMW and the other was a black Cadillac Escalade she couldn't readily identify. Why had Kendra brought someone else with her? Kendra knew how funny she was about that kind of thing.

Dixyn beeped her horn. Simultaneously, Kendra stepped out from the passenger's side of the unknown vehicle while B-Dub exited from the driver's side with a knapsack in his hand. Dixyn wasn't prepared for this.

The mere sight of B-Dub angered her. She was furious at herself for letting Kendra con her into meeting up.

Dixyn stepped out of her car and began to remove her daughter from the safety of her car seat. From the corner of her eye she could see both B-Dub and Kendra walking toward her. Dixyn placed her daughter down and then moved toward the duo.

"Ava," B-Dub said excitedly, as if he knew her.

The little girl stood there with a confused look on her face, clinging to her mother's leg, refusing to greet this stranger.

"Ava, c'mere, girl," Kendra said, trying to diffuse the awkward moment.

The child ran over to Kendra and leaped into her arms. "Kenny!" Ava squealed as Kendra smothered her with kisses.

"Hey, Ava, I'm your uncle. My name is Uncle Brian," B-Dub announced.

Ava was too preoccupied with Kendra to even consider responding to this stranger.

"So, what so important that y'all had to come to my place? Huh?" Dixyn asked.

Kendra calmly put Ava down and looked Dixyn square in the eye. "Fonda and Chocolate are dead."

"What?" Dixyn gasped. "What do you mean dead? How? Why?"

"Like I said, dead. Deceased. Passed away. No longer amongst the living."

Dixyn covered her mouth in shock. Although she didn't particularly like Fonda or Chocolate, she wouldn't wish death on anybody. The news had caught her completely off guard. "Well, how the hell did they die?" she asked.

"The cops ain't really sayin' much, but word on the street is that they got killed. They got run off a back road into a ditch, and the car they was driving burst into flames. So if the crash ain't kill 'em, then the fire did. Word on the street is it wasn't an accident."

What a horrific way to die, Dixyn thought to herself. "What's that supposed to mean?"

"Someone wanted them dead. It was a hit."

Dixyn stared at Kendra as if she didn't comprehend what she was saying.

Kendra continued, "We been movin' around from motel to motel for the last few days, just in case what they say is true. It's harder to hit a movin' target—"

"We came over here to let you know what's up," B-Dub interrupted. "There may be some foul shit goin' on; no one knows for sure yet. We wanted you to be safe, just in case, 'cause we all in this together."

Dixyn considered what they had just told her. One thing she knew for sure was that she had to move wisely. For a few precious moments, no one said anything.

Suddenly Dixyn broke the silence: "I'm callin' the cops." She was beginning to pay close attention to that small voice inside her that was telling her to do something before the same fate befell her. Dixyn was bluffing. Bryce had groomed her against talking to the police, so she didn't plan on contacting any law-enforcement officials if she didn't have to. Still, she had to make it clear to both B-Dub and Kendra that calling the police wasn't out of the realm of possibility.

"You don't wanna do that, fam," B-Dub said. "Remember, we still have that little problem wit' the police ourselves. So if you contact them, that will only draw attention to us and the incident that we were involved in. They'll ask questions that are designed to catch people in lies."

"Well, I don't have anything to hide!" Dixyn shot back.

"Fam, you think 'cause you didn't pull the trigger that you didn't have anything to do with it? Think again. You're an accomplice. This is a commonwealth state, in case you didn't know. In eye of the law in the state of Virginia, you're as guilty as the triggerman. Once they shit you with that conspiracy charge, you goin' down hard, just like the rest of us. So you better think about li'l Ava here before you do somethin' stupid."

"B-Dub," Dixyn replied, allowing a concerned expression to cross her face, "you may not know this, but the police tend to notice when people start dying all over the place. So what are we supposed to do, wait till one of us gets killed?"

"Right now ain't the time to be arguing over this matter," Kendra said. "We need to put our heads together and try to think our way up outta this shit. We should all just lay low up in your house for a couple days, Dixyn, just to get our minds right."

Dixyn didn't like the idea of having B-Dub or Kendra in her home. Under the circumstances, though, she had little choice. She couldn't think of a better option at the moment. So she resigned herself to the thought that she would be able to keep a close eye on these two, if nothing else.

After contemplating the move for a few moments, Dixyn had only one question. "Y'all only going to be here for a few days, right?"

For the next few days, Dixyn reluctantly played hostess to B-Dub and Kendra, cooking, cleaning, and making sure everyone was comfortable. However, keeping them comfortable made Dixyn feel like a prisoner in her own home. She was at their beck and call, and she couldn't eat or sleep right. The situation surrounding their stay had really bothered her.

Although Kendra was her friend and B-Dub was her child's blood uncle, Dixyn made a conscious effort to always keep an eye on her daughter. She didn't trust B-Dub as far as she could throw him, family or no family. And Kendra's drug habit put her in the same category for Dixyn.

"If anybody tries to take you anywhere, just start screamin' your head off," Dixyn coached her daughter in the confines of her bedroom.

"Why, Mommy?" Ava asked innocently.

"'Cause I said so," Dixyn snapped. "Now do as I say, you hear!" She didn't like coming down hard on her daughter like that, but under the circumstances she thought she was doing what was best.

"Yes, Mommy."

Together, the trio of adults sat in the house for hours on end, trying to cook up lies and make up alibis just in case one thing led to another and they were questioned by the police. To Dixyn, this was like a dress rehearsal for some sort of school play, except the results of this production had real-life implications. If their lies weren't believable, this whole thing could blow up in their faces, resulting in prison time for everyone.

The one good thing that came out of their self-imposed seclusion was that it seemed to curtail Kendra's drug habit. Dixyn hadn't seen her so clean in a long time, probably since high school. It may have been a less-than-ideal circumstance in which to kick her habit, yet Dixyn was still happy that she was seizing the opportunity.

But one morning Kendra suddenly snapped. "Yo, I can't take this shit no more. I'm bored out of my fuckin' mind in this place. I'm goin' back to the club tonight."

"You wildin' right now, fam," B-Dub said. "You not bored, bitch. Keep it real, you wanna get high. Who you think you foolin', Kendra? You hooked on that shit so bad you willin' to risk ya freedom or ya life for it."

"You don't know what the fuck you talkin' 'bout!" Kendra shot back. "Nigga, I don't know about you, but I can't stay cooped up in my own house, let alone someone else's, for this long. I'm not a homebody. I needs to be out and about."

Dixyn's eyes darted between the two. Witnessing a spat between Kendra and B-Dub was a first for her. These two conniving lowlifes always seemed to be in cahoots about everything. Dixyn didn't bother to interject her own thoughts, since she wanted them both out of her house anyway. However she achieved this goal was fine with her, whether they took off one at a time or together.

Kendra was adamant about leaving. She looked B-Dub straight in his eye. "Look, muthafucka, I'm grown. I do what the fuck I wanna do, when I wanna do it. I don't gotta explain shit to you or nobody else. I'm tired of hidin' out from some imaginary bogeyman. What's gonna happen is gonna happen. I'm out. Deuces!"

"Kendra, ya fuckin' crazy. You a dead woman walkin' if you go back to that fuckin' club," B-Dub warned. "Bitch, ya best bet is to keep ya ass here and lay low."

"Suck my dick!" Kendra spat. "You stay ya scared ass here. I'm leavin'. My time is up. Bye, Dixyn. Thanks for everything. Call me."

"Okay, fam, go right ahead, it's ya funeral," B-Dub stated.

Kendra glared at him one last time before gathering up her things and exiting the house.

"She's fuckin' crazy! Kendra might as well kiss her ass goodbye," B-Dub mused. "You and I, Dixyn, we gotta be smarter than that, fam. We in this shit together."

Although Dixyn didn't bother to verbalize her thoughts, the feeling was strangely mutual. B-Dub was her lifeline. There was no way she was going to lose sight of that fact, especially now, not until she found out what exactly was going on. Dixyn was doing the only thing she could do in this situation: she sat back and awaited whatever news came their way. So far they had heard nothing—nothing from the street, and nothing from the police.

In the days that followed, Dixyn and Ava had no choice but to interact more with B-Dub. One morning while the three grown-ups were in the living room watching TV, Ava busied herself playing on the floor with a ball. When it rolled over near B-Dub, Ava went to retrieve it. As soon as she got within arm's reach of her uncle, he scooped her up into his arms. And almost instantly, Ava began kicking and screaming in midair, as if she had lost her mind.

"Mommy, Mommy!" she shouted. "Put me down!"

Dixyn pretended to be shocked by her daughter's re-action. But she wasn't. She was proud that Ava had done exactly what she'd been told to do.

A perplexed expression suddenly adorned B-Dub's face. "Dixyn, what's wrong with this kid? She's buggin' out."

"She don't like people picking her up," Dixyn re-plied. "Especially strangers."

"I see."

Ava's thrashing increased until finally she freed her-self. As soon as she hit the ground, she bolted over to her mother's protective arms. From across the room, she glared at her uncle.

"That kid needs to socialize with other people more often. There's no reason for her to act like that," B-Dub remarked.

"Yeah, I know."

"You too overprotective, that child is spoiled."

"Well, you know what they say: a spoiled child is a loved child," Dixyn countered.

"Could you get me a towel?" B-Dub asked, obviously trying to change the subject. "I'm tryin' to take a shower."

Dixyn went upstairs to the linen closet and returned with a fluffy white towel and matching washcloth. "Here," she said, handing him the towel.

"Good lookin', fam," he remarked as he headed to the shower.

Dixyn hoped like hell that B-Dub wasn't up to anything, especially not a repeat performance of his attempted rape. Dixyn told herself she'd kill him if he ever pulled a stunt like that again. This rang even truer with her daughter present in the house. To B-Dub's credit thus far, he hadn't given Dixyn any indication that he was up to his usual tricks. He had been on his best behavior.

As soon as Dixyn heard the bathroom door close and the water begin to run, she turned her attention to B-Dub's knapsack. This was the opportunity she'd been waiting for. She had been studying his habits for days now. He liked to take long, hot showers. Dixyn knew she had an ample amount of time once she heard the shower running.

She was expecting to find drugs or maybe a gun in his bag. What she saw instead totally astonished her. Dixyn found multiple birth certificates and documents from various banks and financial institutions in different names. It appeared to be related to fraud and identity theft. As she studied the documents, she whipped out her phone and began taking pictures of it all. She stored every alias and address in her phone for safekeeping. Just in case this information might come in handy one day. She couldn't help but think how right she had been about him all along: she'd always felt there was more than meets the eye when it came to B-Dub. Now Dixyn had to call into question everything she'd thought she knew, especially all the fancy cars she'd seen him driving. Maybe the automobiles were either stolen or leased, probably the latter. Whatever the case might be, she was now certain he didn't own any of them.

B-Dub was more cunning and conniving than Dixyn had ever given him credit for. She was beginning to understand how he truly operated. Seeing was not believing with him. B-Dub didn't use smoke and mirrors to deceive people. He could fool the average person because they thought with their eyes. All he needed was a nice car, nice clothes, and a pocketful of money—this was enough to make most people believe whatever it was he was saying.

"Mommy," Ava suddenly called out, "what'cha doin'?"

"Shhhh!" Dixyn said, placing her finger across her lips. "Go back in your room and watch TV. Mommy be right there."

Dixyn carefully slipped the documents back inside and set the bag just as she'd found it, then headed to her daughter's room, pretending to have been there the entire time.

Dixyn heard B-Dub's footsteps as he descended the stairs. She and Ava came out of the bedroom and sat down together at the computer. Dixyn logged on to the games website that Ava liked. She waited anxiously for a few moments as her daughter played, half expecting to hear B-Dub scream her name. When that didn't happen, she finally exhaled.

Kendra opened her mouth wide and dumped a molly inside. She washed the pill down with a swig of spring water then left the club early, careful not to bump into anyone from management. Her mind was focused on getting home and getting high.

Quickly she walked across the packed parking lot, seeing nothing but empty vehicles. She noticed a single car idling in the distance. Then she glimpsed a faint glint of the parking lot lights reflected off a chrome-plated gun sticking out of the car's window. She froze in her tracks and was immediately doused by a pair of high beams.

What the fuck is going on? she wondered. *Is this a robbery?*

Kendra squinted in an attempt to get a better look at the gunman, but there was too much light upon her to see much of anything. No matter who it was or why they were there, this couldn't be good. Kendra was trapped, not close enough to easily get to her car and too far away from the club to run back to safety.

As she weighed her options, a single gunshot rang out and a bullet lodged directly into her forehead as her body crumpled to the ground.

* * *

Dixyn thought she was dreaming when she heard a knock on her bedroom door. When the light rapping turned into a hard pounding she stirred out of her sleep and grabbed the knife that she kept hidden beneath her pillow. She looked down at Ava, who was still sound asleep, and slowly advanced toward the door.

"Who's there?" Dixyn groggily called out.

"It's me, B-Dub. Open the door, it's important."

"What is it?" Dixyn huffed.

"Open the door," he repeated. "No funny shit, I swear. I ain't gonna do nuttin' to you, fam. That's my word."

Dixyn slowly unlocked the door and positioned herself behind it, just in case B-Dub tried to surprise her with something.

As the door swung open, B-Dub whispered to her, "Kendra's dead."

"What?" Dixyn exclaimed.

"Kendra's dead. She got killed outside the club in the parking lot. One of the bouncers just called me."

"Did they catch who did it?"

"No, nobody saw nuttin', fam," B-Dub answered gloomily. "It was only one gunshot, so no one really paid it no mind. The bouncer thought it was a car backfiring. Kendra's body was discovered by a customer leaving the place."

Maybe this was karma, Dixyn thought. God only knew who Kendra may have fucked over for some drugs, or maybe she'd rung up a big debt supplying her habit.

The atmosphere inside the house changed dramatically. Fear spread throughout the place like a cold chill on predawn winter morning. And fear wasn't something Dixyn handled well. Her home had been transformed from a safe haven into a death trap. She had to get out of town *now*.

"I'm gone," Dixyn announced. "At least till I find out exactly what's goin' on, I'm leavin' town."

"Oh yeah?" B-Dub replied. "I'm goin' wit' you."

Dixyn didn't even bother to protest. She quickly packed a few things, grabbed her daughter, and hurried out of the house with B-Dub in tow.

CHAPTER TWELVE

Dixyn breathed a huge sigh of relief once they arrived safely at her mother's house deep in the countryside. B-Dub had been totally silent the entire ride there, a welcome nondistraction. She needed the peace and quiet to process everything that had happened and what she planned to do about it. Together they quietly entered the pitch-black house. With her sleeping daughter in her arms, Dixyn led B-Dub to the living room, where he took a seat. Then, after placing Ava in a bed, she began strategically turning on lights in different parts of the house where she felt a forced entrance could possibly occur. Dixyn began entertaining wild thoughts of all them being slaughtered in a violent home invasion. Fear was consuming her.

After Dixyn checked and rechecked all the windows, she returned to the front door. She turned the top lock and listened as the cylinder clicked with a loud thud. Then she slid the chain lock into place. Entering the living room, she found B-Dub slumped low on the sofa, resting his head on a cushion, his eyes pointed at the ceiling.

"That's it," Dixyn barked as B-Dub's eyes slowly came to rest on her. "I'm goin' to the police when I wake up. Too many people are dying around us. And by all indications we're next."

"Here you go wit' that shit again. Look, fam, don't do that," B-Dub said. "You'll only create more problems."

"You don't seem to understand that we're in a life-or-death situation. Do one of us have to die before you realize that something is going on around us? I don't know about you, but I'm not willing to take a chance like that. I, for one, got more at stake here than my life. I got my daughter to think about."

"Listen, it don't have to be like this. We could—"

"I don't wanna hear it!" Dixyn snapped. "Nothing needs to be said. Something needs to be done. I'm not tryin' to hear nothing else."

Dixyn moved into the bedroom where she'd put Ava and locked the door behind her. This door was her last line of defense against whatever evils lurked outside or inside the house. For extra security, she placed the knife that she had tucked into her waistband beneath a pillow— just in case B-Dub wasn't on his best behavior.

For the next several hours, Dixyn remained alert for any noise that went bump in the night inside or outside the house. She felt good about the decision she had made to contact the police, and no matter what B-Dub had to say about the matter, this time she planned on sticking to it.

Finally, in the wee hours of the morning, sleep over-took her, allowing her mind and body an escape from the horrors that had been plaguing her waking hours.

Dixyn had slept through her internal alarm clock. She pried one eye open and peeked at the clock on the night-stand. It read 10:30 a.m. Normally by this time of morn-ing she would have already been awakened by Ava, who would be asking for breakfast or a cartoon.

Second by second, Dixyn came to her senses. Her body began to stretch and yawn. Then it suddenly hit her: Ava was gone. Dixyn rolled over and glanced at the spot next to her where her child was supposed to be. She saw nothing but crumpled sheets and an imprint where her daughter had slept. Dixyn trained her eyes on the bedroom door and saw that it was slightly ajar. *Maybe Ava went to the bathroom or something*, she thought. Dixyn listened for signs of life around the house: the television, a toilet flushing, anything. Instead she heard an eerie silence.

Dixyn jumped out of bed and raced into the living room, which was empty. She frantically searched the en-tire house, yielding nothing. B-Dub and Ava were gone. All she found was the wire hanger that B-Dub had used to unlock the door while she slept.

Dixyn began to weep as she imagined B-Dub drag-ging Ava out of bed while he muffled her cries with a hand over her mouth. In her mind, Ava kicked and screamed all the way to the car. (In all actuality, the child hadn't; B-Dub had removed her from the bed while both mother and child were sound asleep. Once Ava came to, B-Dub had forcibly given the child a strengthy dose of codeine, which put her right back to sleep.)

Dixyn was overcome by a rush of adrenaline mixed with her fear. She couldn't believe B-Dub's audacity. He had hit her in her most vulnerable spot. Dixyn would die if something happened to her daughter. And now there was no way she could go to the police without placing her daughter's life in danger. *This situation spawned from my need to go to the police in the first place,* Dixyn mused. B-Dub clearly didn't like the idea, and was taking preventive measure to ensure that wouldn't happen.

At that moment, Dixyn heard her phone ring. She ran to the bedroom and snatched her cell off the charger without looking at the caller ID. "Bring back my daughter!" she yelled into the phone.

"Oh, you're up now? Huh, fam?" he calmly replied. "You really ought to do something about your sleeping condition. You sleep too hard."

"Look, don't fuckin' play wit' me. Bring back my goddamn daughter or . . ." Dixyn's voice trailed off.

"Or what, Dixyn? In case you haven't noticed, you're in no position to be issuin' any threats, fam. Real talk!"

Even if Dixyn wouldn't admit it out loud, she acknowledged to herself that his statement was totally true. She was more vulnerable to B-Dub's bullshit than ever.

"Now listen up, fam, and listen good. If you ever want to see ya daughter, my niece, alive again, keep ya mouth shut and don't go to the cops. Or you and ya daughter could end up like Kendra, Fonda, and Chocolate."

"You mean to tell me you had something do with them gettin' killed?" Dixyn demanded.

"Why, of course," B-Dub responded. "If I wanted you dead, you woulda been dead a long time ago. I got big plans for you, Dixyn. Together we're goin' to break my poor brother's heart. Them chicks wore out they usefulness."

It finally dawned on Dixyn that she was but a pawn in some sick game between Bryce and his brother. "Okay, okay. I won't go to the police. Just promise me you won't harm my baby. You have my word on that. If you would just bring Ava back, it'll be a done deal."

"Your word ain't good enough!" B-Dub spat. "How do I know you won't change ya mind? I think I'll hold on to ya kid for a li'l while longer to give ya ass something to think about."

The line went dead.

Dixyn tried calling him back a dozen times but could only reach his voice mail. Thoughts of Ava dominated her mind. She took a deep breath, held it in for a few seconds, and then blew it out with a loud sigh. *I gotta pull it together. Stop all this crying shit and think!*

Dixyn knew that even though she had agreed not to go to the police, she wasn't out of the woods yet. She knew her cooperation would probably never be enough—B-Dub would likely either betray or kill her the first chance he got. And now there was only one solution. It was time to take revenge.

From this point on, Dixyn swore to herself, everything she did would be guided by a purpose and a plan.

* * *

Dixyn had no memory of leaving her mother's house and getting in the car. Her eyes couldn't focus on the road, and although she drove for miles, everything she saw was a blur. Dixyn was on a mission. She had one thing on her mind and one thing only: getting her daughter back. Mindlessly, she steered her car into a parking space in the strip mall.

Dixyn walked the short distance to the pawnshop. As soon as she entered the premises, the owner spotted her. He remembered her face. There was no way he would forget it, not after the way she had cursed him out. The incident was still fresh in his mind. He watched closely as Dixyn walked straight over to him.

"How can I help you, ma'am?"

Dixyn looked straight in his eye without uttering a single word.

"Ma'am? How can I help you?" he repeated.

"I'm looking to buy a gun," she responded. "Do you have any?"

"Well, of course we do. What kind are you looking for? A high-caliber firearm? Or maybe something smaller?"

"I don't care, just as long as it holds a lot of bullets." Dixyn didn't know exactly what she would do if she found B-Dub. But she would arm herself just in case things got ugly. She only knew that, given the situation, she was doing what any parent would do, and that was going to New York City to find her child.

CHAPTER THIRTEEN

Dixyn drove nonstop through the night on I-95 and then the New Jersey Turnpike to New York City. The frustration of not being able to adequately provide for her daughter, then not being able to protect her, festered in her mind. Every minute she spent away from Ava was killing her. She wondered how B-Dub was treating her, what he was feeding her, and where she was sleeping. She thought about the terrible things that could possibly be happening to her.

For the entirety of the ride, Dixyn's imagination ran wild as she considered just how B-Dub had gotten her to lower her guard. While she and her daughter were fast asleep, B-Dub had been wide awake in the living room, plotting and scheming. *His devious mind must have been working overtime*, Dixyn mused. He must have patiently waited an hour or two before executing his plan. Now his words turned out to be prophetic: *There's a lotta different ways of hurtin' a person without gettin' physical*. The words echoed in her ears. B-Dub had taken away almost everything she held near and dear on this earth. Now Dixyn wanted it back.

After the fact, Dixyn had discovered the broken hanger that B-Dub had used to unlock the bedroom door. Yet she still wondered how he had been able to leave the premises without stealing a vehicle. Thanks to an old security camera that her mother had had installed on her porch a long time ago—after her home was broken into while she was on vacation—Dixyn was able to find the answer.

She had gone into her mother's bedroom and replayed the surveillance footage from that morning. On the small monitor, Dixyn watched grainy black-and-white footage that showed a dark-colored SUV with New York license plates, driven by a female, pulling up into her yard and B-Dub exiting the house carrying her sleeping daughter. So there it was, clear as day.

Dixyn had pulled out her phone and punched in the first New York address she'd recorded from B-Dub's mysterious documents. Common sense told her to check out all the New York addresses; B-Dub had to reside at one of these places. At least she hoped. At this point, hope was all she had. So she headed to New York on a wing and a prayer.

Now that she was able to really think about it as she drove north, she saw how B-Dub thrived on keeping whomever he dealt with off balance. If one couldn't predict what he was going to do next, then one couldn't mount a defense against him.

B-Dub must have thought that New York City was big enough for him to hide in. But as clever as he had been in the execution of his treacherous plan, Dixyn would prove she was equally as shrewd in tracking him down.

She was proud of the way she was keeping calm and was able to figure out a way to track B-Dub down so quickly. And she was hoping the element of surprise would be on her side. She hoped that B-Dub had underestimated her. In fact, she counted on it. Dixyn promised herself one thing: whenever they met again, B-Dub would see a side of her that he had never even glimpsed.

Dixyn interpreted her daughter's kidnapping as the latest trial in a short period of her life filled with trials to determine exactly what she was made of. If this was indeed a test, Dixyn planned on passing with flying colors. She intended to put an end to B-Dub's bullshit once and for all.

More than her innate maternal instinct to find and protect her child, it was the desire for revenge that drove Dixyn to New York City to come face to face with a murderer on unfamiliar grounds. So while most of the other drivers on the highway obeyed the speed limit, Dixyn blatantly defied it. She had somewhere to be, and time was of the essence.

One by one she staked out the half-dozen or so addresses scattered across the city. Dixyn saw no sign of B-Dub or that dark SUV. As time passed, she grew more frantic in her search for her baby. Then suddenly it dawned on her: Bryce and B-Dub were from Spanish

Harlem. Dixyn felt she would be better off looking there. She went back inside her phone, and sure enough, there was a Spanish Harlem adress. Dixyn punched it in her GPS and quickly raced up there.

Inside a decrepit tenement building on 110th Street and Lexington Avenue, B-Dub relaxed with a female friend. Camilla exhaled a huge cloud of smoke and watched as it slowly dissolved into thin air. Now that her on-again/off-again boyfriend B-Dub was back in town, her routine was about to change—at least until he disappeared once more.

B-Dub lived in limbo between New York and whatever town or city he was hustling in. No matter how good he had it, he always returned home, especially when things went bad and he needed to regroup.

"Here, take a hit of this shit. It's good," she insisted, extending the blunt toward B-Dub. "It'll git ya mind right."

B-Dub sat on the sofa just a few feet away, too preoccupied with surfing the Internet on his iPhone to hear what she was saying. Refusing to be ignored, Camilla waved the blunt in his face.

"Yo, git that shit outta my face, fam," he growled, pushing her hand away. "You know I don't git high."

"C'mon, why you gotta be like that?" she said. "Just do it for me." There was nothing that Camilla liked more than having sex while she was high. Smoking weed made her three things—high, hungry, and horny. She was beginning to wonder who else he might be fucking. B-Dub rarely, if ever, turned down an opportunity to have sex with her.

"Camilla, you violating right now," he warned. "I said no."

Reluctantly, she pulled her hand back and continued taking tokes on the blunt. Although she was mad as hell, she tried hard not to show it. She knew an argument would kill her high. The problems she was having with B-Dub were bigger than a blunt.

Their relationship pattern always seemed to favor B-Dub. He came around when he wanted to and stayed away when he didn't want to be bothered with her. Long ago, Camilla began to worry that this thing of theirs was merely a relationship of convenience. He was there for her financially whenever she fell behind on her bills or just needed a few dollars. She was there for him whenever he needed a place to rest his head or lay low. Whenever he needed sex, there were no strings attached and no questions asked.

Camilla had a particular skill set in the bedroom that B-Dub had come to favor. Her oral talents were like no other woman who B-Dub had ever met. For that reason alone, he always returned to Camilla no matter how far away he had strayed. Truth be told, she hated him running in and out of her life. She always wondered where he had been, what he'd been doing, and who he'd been sleeping with. His behavior was so erratic that there were times when she didn't even know if he was dead or alive. All she knew was that whenever he did return to New York, he was always flush with cash and driving an expensive car. And B-Dub wasn't one to speak his business or bring the streets to her door. But judging from the large amounts of cash that he always carried on him, it was definitely something illegal.

"Let's fuck," Camilla blurted out.

Oblivious, B-Dub continued to do whatever he was doing on his phone. He didn't even bother to look up at her.

"Damn, man, what the fuck!" she cried out. "What a bitch gotta do to get your attention? Shit!"

B-Dub diverted his eyes from his phone and shot her an evil glare. "I'm out!" he spat. As he rose to his feet, he felt a little light-headed from the secondhand weed smoke.

"If you don't mind me asking, where the hell you going?"

B-Dub knew there was a difference between a female being nosy and being genuinely concerned. Right now, Camilla was just being plain nosy, and B-Dub wasn't feeling her.

"Yes, I do mind you askin'," he countered. "I'm grown, fam. I pay ya bills; you don't pay mine. Just know this: I'll be gone for a while, but I'll be back. That's all you need to know."

Camilla sucked her teeth. "So you just gon' leave me here by myself, huh?"

"You couldn't come even if I wanted you to!" he barked. "You forgettin' somethin', fam. Who the hell is gonna watch my niece who's sleepin' in ya bed?"

Shit! Camilla had totally forgotten about that. She

kicked herself mentally for agreeing to watch the child in the first place. Although she didn't voice it, she had her suspicions about the girl. She could just as easily have been his love child as his so-called niece. Although there was a vague resemblance between the two, Camilla had to wonder what person in their right mind would leave a child in the care of B-Dub.

He had brought some strange things to her house before: shady characters, money, guns. However, a child for her to watch was a first. All he'd said was that she was his niece, and he left it at that. True to form, he hadn't bothered to explain what she was doing with him or how long she would even be there. Not wanting to rock the boat, Camilla had just gone along with the situation. She'd asked him no questions and he'd told her no lies.

"So what am I supposed to do in the morning if you're not here when she wakes up hungry and there's nothing here to fix her? Huh?"

Standing by the front door, B-Dub dug in his pockets and removed a wad of money. He took out two twenties and handed them to her. "Whatever you do," he warned, "don't feed that little girl no pork. You hear me, fam?"

"Yeah, okay," she responded. Then: "B, you one funny nigga. You eat pussy, yet you worried 'bout someone bu-yin' some pork wit' ya damn money."

B-Dub didn't find Camilla's attempt at humor funny at all and simply walked out of the apartment. He knew that would hurt her more than anything.

"Fuck you!" she shouted after him.

* * *

Having traveled through the night, Dixyn arrived in the city just in time to get a taste of the snarling rush hour. After being stuck in bumper-to-bumper traffic the entire way through the Lincoln Tunnel, Dixyn drove the streets to her Spanish Harlem destination.

Dixyn took stock of her new surroundings. The first thing she noticed about New York at this time of day was that it was extremely noisy. She had lived in a small town in Virginia most of her life where there were ordinances against noise pollution. It seemed like every sound she heard here was amplified, from car horns to the casual pedestrian conversations. Dixyn was also leery of New York City from all the horror stories about tourists who found themselves in harm's way after taking a wrong turn. She was determined to leave this city as she had come, and not turn into a statistic. Dixyn kept her eyes open and her mouth shut, observing everything around her.

When she finally arrived, she glanced down at the address on the GPS, checking it against the numerals that hung on the building's entrance, then found a parking space with a good view. Before she doing anything rash, she decided to conduct some surveillance of her own on the building, monitoring its residents' comings and goings. Her visual senses began to sharpen as everyone she saw fell under suspicion. Anything that moved in or out of that building, she was on.

A man and a small child leaving the building would be easy to spot, even from her current distance. Dixyn also figured that more than likely he had some type of female assistance. As far as she knew, B-Dub didn't have any children of his own. He would need help to properly look after Ava. Whatever the case might be, Dixyn was preparing herself for any scenario.

She didn't know what her next move should be. She could either go knock on the door or wait around till B-Dub showed his face. For now, she decided to wait it out. But as badly as she wanted her daughter back, she didn't know how long she could exercise such restraint.

As Ava awoke from her sleep, she looked around the room in confusion. This wasn't her room; this wasn't her grandmother's house. She didn't remember much about her abduction because B-Dub had slipped her a sedative to shut her up. Finally the effects had worn off, but little Ava still didn't know where she was. She got scared and started crying, and stumbled off the bed. It took her a few steps to get her legs under her. She began the survey the place for any signs of life. It didn't take long before she came across Camilla lying on the couch, all but dead to the world.

"I want my mom," Ava said as she tapped the stranger on the leg. "Where's my mommy? I'm hungry."

Camilla startled awake and realized she must have fallen asleep on the couch after smoking that last blunt. "Little girl, stop hitting me, I'm up!" she shouted. "I'm up."

"Where's my mommy? I'm hungry!" Ava cried.

Camilla sat up on the couch, leaned forward, and looked the girl directly in the eye. She tried her best to be nice, but she was agitated after being woken so abruptly. "Look, little girl, I don't know who your mother is or where she's at, but your uncle will be back soon. Now if you stop crying I'll get you something to eat." She started gently wiping the tears away from the little girl's face. Ava began to calm down.

Camilla called the local Spanish takeout restaurant and ordered the special: a whole chicken with rice, beans, and plantains. "We gonna eat in a little while, okay?" she explained to Ava. "The food is on the way." Camilla picked up the television remote and changed the channel to the Cartoon Network, then went in the kitchen and made the child a bag of microwave popcorn.

She handed Ava the treat and the little girl began to stuff her face. "Damn, you really was hungry, huh? Girl, you sure fucking that popcorn up."

With the child momentarily quiet, Camilla grabbed a bag of weed that was hidden in her bra, and reached over to the coffee table and grabbed a blunt wrap and began rolling. *This is the way to start your day,* Camilla thought to herself.

No sooner had she taken her first puff of her blunt than she began peppering the little girl with all sorts of questions in a childlike voice, questions that she didn't dare ask B-Dub.

As the morning wore on, Dixyn grew increasingly impatient with this cat-and-mouse game. She'd had enough of sitting, waiting, and watching. With phone in hand, she sprang into action. Dixyn exited her car, making sure she locked the doors, and made her way to the building's front door, which was not secured. She cautiously navigated the steps toward the second-floor apartment, constantly looking over her shoulder as if she were expecting B-Dub to suddenly appear at any moment. Before she even reached the apartment door, she was overcome by a strong scent of weed.

Dixyn ignored it and knocked on the apartment door. She slipped her own phone inside her bag and stepped away from the door, out of view of the peephole, pressing her body up against the wall. With her hand still inside the bag, Dixyn gripped her gun and waited for someone to answer the door.

"Who?" a female voice called out from within the apartment.

Camilla was so high that she might have thought she heard a response. Either that or she now remembered that a delivery guy was supposed to be bringing her food. Whatever the case, Camilla unhooked the door chain without even looking out the peephole.

Dixyn stepped in front of the door as soon as she heard the locks being unbolted.

"You're not the delivery guy. Who are you?" Camilla looked suspiciously at the unfamiliar beauty standing at her door.

"Excuse me, I'm lookin' for B-Dub," Dixyn replied. "Is he in there?"

Camilla immediately put two and two together and concluded that Dixyn must be the little girl's mother. Realizing this was a chance to get in good with B-Dub, she decided to play stupid. "Who's that? I don't know who you're talking about."

Just as Dixyn was about to challenge the lie, a small child came from behind the door and clung to the woman's leg. Dixyn looked down just as the child looked up.

"Mommy?"

Angrily, Dixyn pulled out her handgun, placed the barrel to Camilla's head, and shoved her way inside the apartment.

The sound of the lock cylinder turning alerted Dixyn to someone else's presence. According to Camilla, who she had tied up and interrogated at gunpoint, B-Dub was due back anytime now. Dixyn had intercepted the delivery man, who came to the door to bring the food just like B-Dub's girlfriend told her he would. So if Camilla was to indeed be believed, this mysterious person about to gain entrance to the apartment was none other than B-Dub himself.

After the door slammed shut, Dixyn heard faint footsteps approaching. The way the apartment was designed, whoever it was coming down the hallway would have to pass the living room to get to the other rooms. It was there in the darkness of the living room that Dixyn lay in wait, ready to ambush her prey.

"Yo, Camilla!" a man called out from down the hall. "Where the hell are you?"

There was no mistaking that voice. Dixyn had endured the unpleasantness of it so many times that she could recognize it in her sleep.

The closer the footsteps came the louder they grew, until finally B-Dub was upon her. Dixyn began to tense up at the sight of him. She gripped her gun tightly, watching and waiting.

In the pitch blackness of the living room, B-Dub squinted, struggling to make out the form that sat motionless on the couch. Without appearing to give it any thought, he flipped on the light. If he was taken by surprise by the presence of Dixyn, B-Dub didn't show it. His lips creased in a sly smile.

Dixyn locked her eyes onto the man. "Didn't expect to see me here, now did you? You're not as hard to find as you may think."

"I see," he responded calmly. "I underestimated you."

"That you did." In one swift motion, Dixyn sprang up off the couch and leveled her weapon at B-Dub. "Ava, dear, please go to the bathroom," she instructed, and the little girl quickly complied.

Now B-Dub became visibly upset, and his smile turned into a frown. "Look, fam, put the gun down and let's talk this thing out. This whole situation was a misunderstandin'. I thought you were goin' to turn me in to the police. That's the only reason why I did what I did. Ava's my niece, my blood. Did you really think I was goin' to hurt her?"

Dixyn remained silent. She could care less what he had to say.

He continued, "I know this might sound crazy, but all I ever tried to do was look out for you, hold you down, be your friend, fam."

"Friend?" Dixyn cried in disbelief.

"C'mon, fam. I know our signals somehow got crossed, but if it wasn't for me, you wouldn't still have that house or that car."

"And if it wasn't for you, I wouldn't have a murder charge possibly hanging over my head. And if it wasn't for you, my friend Kendra wouldn't be dead, not to mention a whole lotta other people. And if it wasn't for you, I wouldn't be stressed the fuck out, way up here in New York City, going half-crazy looking for my fuckin' child. I don't know what kinda sick vendetta you got against ya brother, but I wish you hadn't involved me or my daughter in it!"

Dixyn was glad that her daughter was on the other side of the bathroom door; she didn't want her to witness any of this. And B-Dub's girlfriend was still bound and gagged.

"You're only goin' to make the situation worse," he warned. "It's not worth it, believe me, fam. This is all a big mistake." B-Dub began inching his way toward Dixyn, hoping she wouldn't notice.

But she did. She readjusted her grip and held the gun steady. She was running out of patience and B-Dub was running out of time.

"Dixyn, come on now, put the gun down," he coaxed. Then suddenly he lunged for it.

The gunshot was just an instinctive reaction. Dixyn's mind couldn't fully process what was happening. It was as if everything was taking place in slow-motion. She watched as the projectile flew at him and slammed into his chest, knocking him back a few feet.

Starting when she was a teenager, Dixyn had been trained to shoot firearms in the backwoods of Virginia by her stepfather. That training was serving her well right now. She was not disturbed by the loud report or the kick of the gun. After the weapon recoiled, she repositioned herself, took aim, and prepared to fire again, if need be.

A dead silence enveloped the apartment, though Dixyn could hear her daughter crying in the bathroom.

"You fuckin' bitch! You fuckin' shot me!" B-Dub wheezed as blood flowed freely from a wound in his upper torso. "You gon' pay for this." Enraged, he charged at Dixyn with such ferocity that she thought he had lost his mind. Without fear or hesitation, she let off three more shots in rapid succession. The impact of the bullets propelled B-Dub backward, and he crumpled.

Like a trained assassin, Dixyn cautiously approached her victim as he writhed on the floor.

"Fam, I'm fuckin' bleeding to death . . . Call 911 . . . Get me to a hospital before it's too late."

Dixyn thought about all the humiliation she had endured at the hands of B-Dub: the threat of blackmail, the attempted rape, the abduction of her daughter. Then there were the murders of Kendra and the other two strippers. Her decision was irreversible. She showed no mercy.

"If I were you, I wouldn't worry too much about where I'm goin'. There's only one place *you* can go." Dixyn stood over him, took aim, and squeezed the trigger one last time. "Go to hell, muthafucka!"

Death was Dixyn's only way out of this situation.

She had no remorse whatsoever for what she had just done. In her book, B-Dub deserved to die. She knew that if she'd let him live, showed him leniency, the decision would have come back to haunt her. This was only way it could have ended between them: in a hail of bullets.

EPILOGUE

Dixyn's foray into the world of stripping was fueled by money, or the lack thereof, and while she had good intentions, ultimately it had been a terrible decision. The repercussions were still being felt. Murder was a tough thing for her to digest, especially the murder of Camilla. That was something she would always regret. Although Camilla hadn't harmed Ava in any way, shape, or form, her death was collateral damage. Camilla was just at the wrong place at the wrong time. Had she been left alive, Dixyn would have had to spend the rest of her life looking over her shoulder, waiting for the police to arrest her. Dixyn had killed her in the most painless way possible: she'd held Camilla's head underwater in the tub until the woman, still tied up, stopped struggling and then stopped breathing. With the deaths of Chocolate, Fonda, Kendra, B-Dub, and now Camilla, she was sure that her secrets were now safe.

In light of all the recent drama, Dixyn decided to

push the reset button on her life. Going back to the basics, she rid herself of the town house and the SUV—not because they were symbols of what had happened, but because she could no longer afford such luxuries. Dixyn had been pampered and spoiled by Bryce, and in his absence she'd been forced to stand on her own two feet. Although she hadn't liked the outcome, she enjoyed the sense of empowerment that handling her own business gave her. If she did it once, she could do it again, this time the right way.

She decided to move back home and start from scratch. She discovered that the material possessions she had cherished held no real value in her life anymore. Now she would get the things she needed the old-fashioned way: by working for them. If she didn't earn it, then she didn't want it, end of story. It was all about Ava. Family came first from this point on.

There was one more matter that Dixyn had to address before she could move on, and that was her relationship with her fiancé and his dire legal situation. Dixyn had come clean to Bryce about the stripping and her situation with B-Dub—she'd told him everything except the murders. He responded poorly, just as she thought he would. It was then that Dixyn realized they were moving in opposite directions. She was starting a new life, while he was still answering for the actions of his old life.

While initially Bryce didn't like the decision, over time he learned not only to accept it, but to respect it. After all, he had fifteen years to serve, and that was a very long time by anyone's standards. Together they made a pact to be the best parents they could under the circumstances. She would bring her daughter to visit him whenever time and money allowed. When Bryce got close to being released from prison, they would broach the subject of reconciliation.

For the time being, they would focus on just being friends.

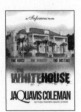